Dalton for Hire

When Dalton holed up in Yellow Creek he tried to put his past behind him. But for a wanted man there can be no peace and he soon finds himself as wealthy Raphael Huffman's hired gun. Now, with a carpet-bag bulging with money to guard in a town bristling with gunslingers, it isn't long before somebody risks Dalton's ever-ready gun.

But Dalton didn't expect the money to be stolen from right under his nose and, even worse, for the prime suspect to be his good friend Ryan Foxglove. Despite the numerous killers standing in his way, Dalton must track down the missing loot to prove Ryan's innocence – and stay out of jail.

Dalton for Hire

Ed Law

A Black Horse Western

ROBERT HALE · LONDON

© Ed Law 2005
First published in Great Britain 2005

ISBN 0 7090 7769 6

Robert Hale Limited
Clerkenwell House
Clerkenwell Green
London EC1R 0HT

Typeset by
Derek Doyle & Associates, Shaw Heath.
Printed and bound in Great Britain by
Antony Rowe Limited, Wiltshire.

CHAPTER 1

Deputy Vaughn was closing.

Twenty yards on from the relentless lawman, Dalton spurred his horse, but his straining mount was already galloping as fast as it could.

Hoofs pounded as Vaughn drew in directly behind Dalton, who hunched forward and, with a mighty shake of the reins, tried to drag one last burst of speed from his horse. But then a tightness gripped around his arms and waist and pulled tight. Dalton looked down to see that Vaughn had lassoed him.

In desperation, he released the reins to grab the rope and tugged, but Vaughn pulled it even tighter as he swung round to flank Dalton.

'Give up, Dalton,' Vaughn shouted, 'or I'll rip you in two.'

For another fifty yards, Dalton rode on, but then grabbed the reins and pulled back. At his side, Vaughn slowed, matching his reducing speed until they'd both halted. But when Vaughn nudged his horse to the side to approach him, Dalton swung round in the saddle, grabbed the rope, and jerked back, aiming to pull Vaughn from his horse.

His sudden action did drag Vaughn to a standing position, but Vaughn flopped back into the saddle and pulled. The two men strained for supremacy, but with the rope feeling as though it was cutting Dalton in two, Vaughn slowly started to drag Dalton from his horse. Then, with his shoulders braced, he ripped Dalton from the saddle. Dalton somersaulted through the air before slamming into the ground on his back.

He rolled twice before coming to a bone-jarring halt on his belly. He threw both his hands up to grip the rope before him, but Vaughn encouraged his horse to break into a trot and dragged him off the trail. Dalton bounced and ripped over the stony ground.

As they approached a gaunt pile of boulders, Vaughn repeatedly glanced over his shoulder to taunt Dalton, but Dalton firmed his jaw and stared up, refusing to let Vaughn bait him.

So Vaughn pulled back on the reins, then dismounted. As he paced round to confront him, Dalton staggered to his feet and struggled, trying to free his bound arms, but just as he felt the rope give an inch, Vaughn pulled the trailing rope taut.

Dalton shook his shoulders, then lifted his arms at the elbows.

'You got no right arresting me, Vaughn,' he muttered.

'You will call me Deputy Vaughn.' Vaughn swaggered forward. 'Now, drop that gunbelt.'

'I ain't got a gun no more.'

'You might have a hidden knife. So, drop it!'

Dalton wafted his arms, feigning an inability to reach his belt. Vaughn snorted and reached out to remove it himself, but as his hand touched Dalton's waist, Dalton jutted his head forwards, aiming to headbutt Vaughn. He'd aimed for Vaughn's nose, but Vaughn saw the blow coming and jerked his head back. Even so, Dalton's forehead slammed into his cheek and while Vaughn staggered back, Dalton kicked Vaughn's feet from under him and landed him on his back.

Vaughn moved to get up, but Dalton crunched a kick into Vaughn's ribs that sent him rolling. The rope slipped from Vaughn's hand, so Dalton ripped the coils from his chest then kicked Vaughn again, but this time Vaughn lifted with the blow and staggered to his feet. He backed away from Dalton, clutching his guts, then ripped his gun from its holster, but as he swung the weapon up, Dalton kicked out, the toe of his boot hitting the barrel and knocking it from Vaughn's grip.

Even before the gun had wheeled to the ground, Dalton had cracked a huge uppercut to Vaughn's chin that lifted his feet from the ground, then delivered a second pile-driving blow to his cheek which spun him around and slammed him to the dirt. Vaughn slid five feet before coming to a halt.

In an instant, Dalton was on him. He pulled Vaughn's head up and ripped back his fist, ready to slug him the moment he moved, but Vaughn lay supine in his grip. Dalton knelt, poised, but then acknowledged that his opponent was out cold and pushed Vaughn's head to the ground. He felt his neck, confirming that he'd only knocked him unconscious.

He nodded to himself and stood over him, rubbing his ribs, then dragged Vaughn to the rocks and into shade.

With a hand to his brow, he searched the landscape for any potential witnesses to this fight. A solitary rider *was* heading down the trail, but Dalton watched him and confirmed that this man was galloping by and not paying any attention to what was happening off the trail.

When the rider had passed, Dalton rummaged through Vaughn's pockets.

Vaughn had around five dollars, but Dalton gritted his teeth and replaced it. Despite his resolution not to steal Vaughn's money, he secured Vaughn's horse, then removed the saddle. With a huge slap on the rump and much hollering, he spooked it, encouraging it to head off into the plains.

The horse still stopped a few hundred yards away. But to lengthen the time it would take Vaughn to resume his pursuit, he tied Vaughn's hands and feet with the rope – not so tightly that he wouldn't be able to free himself, but enough to slow him.

Then he mounted his horse and galloped to the trail to resume his westward journey. Behind him was Yellow Creek, ahead Ogden.

For the last forty-two days, Dalton had tried every devious trick he could think of to throw Vaughn off his trail, but this time he settled for putting as much distance as he could between himself and his pursuer.

But ten minutes after reaching the trail, he heard a gunshot blast behind him. Dalton gritted his teeth and glanced over his shoulder.

A quarter-mile back a horse was galloping after him. He narrowed his eyes, but the figure was too distant for him to confirm whether it was Vaughn. Dalton dismissed his puzzlement as to how Vaughn had freed himself then regained his horse so quickly, and concentrated on hard riding.

But then, ahead, he saw the rider who had passed him earlier. Even from 200 yards back, he saw that this man's horse was in distress. Its white-coated flanks were straining and the desperate rider was spurring it at every stride, but his efforts weren't stopping his mount from slowing.

Dalton glanced over his shoulder again, sizing up the rapidly approaching rider behind him.

He nodded to himself, accepting that neither man had any connection to Vaughn's pursuit of him. But even so, a man in his position could take no chances. So, when the trail rounded a low hill, he veered off it, taking a rough track to the summit of the hill.

On high, he stopped and looked down. The pursuing rider was gaining fast, but just as he passed the point where Dalton had left the trail, the leading horse's knees buckled, throwing its rider to the ground. The horse skidded on to its side, then struggled to rise but, after a pitiful tremble of the legs and a thrashing of its head, it stilled. The rider rolled back and shook the horse, but even from the top of the hill, Dalton could tell that it was never getting up again.

The following rider bore down on his quarry and, content now that he wasn't pursuing *him*, Dalton headed over the top of the hill. He looked back once and saw that the following rider was chasing the other man into a tangle of rocks. Beside them lay a sharp incline down to a dry wash, but Dalton continued his journey.

Ahead, the rough track cut a route down through a tangle of thickets then back up another low hill.

'That just wasn't my problem,' Dalton whispered under his breath. 'It just wasn't. I got problems of my own.'

He headed to lower ground. From behind him, on the other side of the hill, came raised voices, then a gunshot sounded, followed by more raised voices.

Dalton snorted and rode on, but then pulled his horse to a halt.

With his eyes closed, he listened, hearing another shout. He shrugged then turned his horse and headed back up the hill.

CHAPTER 2

'Take your hands off him,' Dalton said, stepping out from the boulder.

One man lay on the ground before him. The other man had dragged this man up by the collar and had wrenched back his fist, ready to slug his jaw. To their side, two guns lay on the ground.

The standing man flinched and swirled round, releasing his grip to let the other man sprawl on to the ground. He glanced at Dalton's clenched fists, then at his gunbelt.

He snorted. 'Scat. This ain't your concern.'

Dalton raised his fists. 'And I'm making this my concern. Step away, and you'll get no trouble.'

'Stay out of this,' the standing man muttered. 'This is Stirling Kimball and I'm Quentin—'

'Ain't caring what anyone's name is.'

The man on the ground, Stirling, looked up at Dalton, but although Quentin had been roughing him up, he had none of the fear in his eyes that

Dalton expected to see.

But as Quentin swung round to confront Dalton, Stirling kicked out, trying to knock Quentin's legs from under him. His kick only tumbled Quentin forward a pace, but Quentin pivoted on his right leg and swung his left leg around to crunch his boot into the point of Stirling's chin, pole-axing him in a moment.

Dalton took advantage of the distraction to dash towards them. He pounded across the ground and threw himself at Quentin, hitting him in the side and tumbling him on to his back. But Quentin kicked up, using Dalton's momentum to cartwheel him over his head.

Dalton crunched to a halt on the edge of the steep incline to the dry wash. He lay on his back for a moment, shaking his head, then leapt to his feet and swung round to confront his opponent, but it was only to see a vicious right hook swinging at his face. Dalton thrust his head down, the blow went whistling over his head, and the force of the missed blow swung Quentin around.

Taking advantage of Quentin being momentarily off-balance, Dalton lunged forward and grabbed Quentin in a bear-hug. He swung him around so that his back was to him and he faced the incline.

'Let me go,' Quentin whined. He squirmed, but found that Dalton had a strong grip.

'I will.' For emphasis, Dalton pushed Quentin forward a pace so that Quentin had to dig his heels in to avoid tumbling down the slope. 'But only when you stop struggling.'

'You don't know what's at stake here.'

Dalton glanced over his shoulder at Stirling, who was lying flat on the ground, his arms and legs spread wide.

'I recognize an ambush when I see one.'

Quentin snorted, then went limp, but as Dalton shrugged to grip his chest more tightly, Quentin used his small amount of leverage to hammer his elbow back into Dalton's ribs.

The blow hit with sufficient force to blast the air from Dalton's chest and loosen his grip. With a second blow, Quentin shook himself free. Dalton staggered back a pace, thrusting his fists up, ready to defend himself, but Quentin dashed for his gun instead.

Dalton hurtled after him, but Quentin threw himself flat and skidded along the ground, gathering the gun into his grip as he slid by it.

Dalton was two paces behind and, as Quentin rolled to his haunches and swung his gun round to aim it up at him, Dalton reached him and kicked out, aiming to kick the gun away. His flailing foot missed the gun but arced into Quentin's ribs, crunching with a dull thud.

Quentin winced, but then shook off the blow and rolled back on to his feet to confront Dalton.

In desperation, Dalton slammed a round-armed blow to Quentin's cheek that knocked his head back and delivered a sharp uppercut to the chin that made Quentin's legs shake. As Quentin staggered in a circle, his eyes rolling, Dalton kicked his rump, knocking him towards the edge of the incline.

He advanced on Quentin and, in both hands, grabbed Quentin's left arm. With all his might, he hurled him forwards, but Quentin dug his heels in and skidded to a halt. He teetered a moment, but a flat-palmed blow to the back of the head sent him on his way and he slid from sight.

While batting his hands together, Dalton peered over the edge to watch Quentin slide and tumble down the slope in a shower of dirt. He flopped to a halt by the side of the dry river-bottom, halting with his feet dangling in what would be, come the rains, water.

Dalton watched, confirming that Quentin's head lolled, then turned and headed back to Stirling to find that he was now stirring. Dalton still knelt beside him and slapped his face until he opened his eyes.

'Much obliged,' Stirling murmured, rubbing his chin.

'That was no trouble.' Dalton sighed and rolled back on to his haunches. 'It's getting as it just ain't safe for travellers out on the trail.'

'You're right there.' Stirling flexed his jaw, then looked up at Dalton. 'And who is my saviour?'

'Dalton.'

'Just Dalton?'

'Just Dalton.'

Stirling smiled, then licked his lips as he climbed to the feet. He swayed a moment, rubbing his temple, then retrieved his fallen hat, slapped the dust from it, and swung it on to his head.

'That sure does explain a lot.'

'What you mean?'

Stirling shrugged, then picked up his gun. He moved to slip it into his holster, then swirled it in his grip and aimed it at Dalton.

'I mean that a man like you needs to think before he leaps into situations.'

Dalton stared at the gun, then into Stirling's eyes, but on seeing no hope of mercy in either, raised his hands.

'You can't shoot me after I saved you.'

Stirling glanced at the gun, then shrugged.

'I guess I can't. But I need a horse, or I'm going nowhere. And yours will do.' Stirling grinned. 'You can take Quentin's.'

'I don't steal.'

Stirling snorted, then paced backwards from Dalton until he reached his horse. He mounted it, then pranced the horse back a pace and pulled the reins to the side. Then he turned back.

'You heading to Yellow Creek, looking for work?'

'Passed through, then moved on.'

'Well, if you do go back, try the Hotel Splendour. That place needs help.'

'Obliged, I suppose.' Dalton glanced at the edge of the incline. 'And before you steal my horse, tell me one thing – who was your attacker?'

'Quentin.' Stirling chuckled. 'Sheriff Patrick Quentin.'

Stirling turned Dalton's horse towards the trail and headed off, leaving Dalton to slap his hat to the ground, then kick it away.

CHAPTER 3

With his hands on his hips, Dalton sighed and glanced at the sheriff's horse, then back towards the trail.

Soon Vaughn would come for him, but Dalton reckoned he still had a few hours before that pursuit came. So he retrieved his hat and paced down the slope to the sheriff's side.

The lawman was still unconscious, so Dalton hunkered down beside him. He pressed a hand to the river bottom, receiving some coolness from the mud, then laid it on the sheriff's brow. With his other hand, he slapped his cheeks.

The sheriff lay flat, but when Dalton slapped his cheeks with a more insistent rhythm, he stirred.

'What you doing?' the sheriff murmured, batting Dalton's hand away as he opened his eyes. Then, seeing Dalton kneeling over him, he flinched away, but Dalton raised his hands.

'I don't mean you no harm,' Dalton said. 'I'm just checking that you're all right.'

Quentin rubbed the back of his head. 'I guess I am, seeing as you assaulted me.'

'I'm sorry. But I didn't know you were a lawman.'

Quentin shuffled up to a sitting position.

'And this lawman was all set to arrest Stirling Kimball, until you stopped me.'

'I know that now. But what was I supposed to do when I see a man roughing up another man?'

'Ask why before you charge in.'

'When I see a man in trouble, I don't wait around. And you could have said that you were a lawman. Then I . . .' Dalton sighed as Quentin flared his eyes. 'I'll ask next time.'

Quentin lowered his head. 'And I guess you were right. I should have said, but when you're facing an outlaw, you don't have time to answer no questions. And I'm obliged that you didn't run. It stops me chasing you down, too.'

'Had no choice but to stay. Stirling stole my horse.'

'Now, that's gratitude for you.' Quentin moved to rise, but then winced. He held out a hand and Dalton dragged him to his feet. He swayed, but, with a shake of the head and a roll of the shoulders, he regained his composure and paced up the incline. At the top, he peered around. 'Which way did he go?'

Dalton hurried to join Quentin and pointed.

'That-a-way, to the hills.'

Quentin rested a raised leg on the top of the incline and leaned on his knee. He peered down the trail, then over his shoulder and back to Yellow Creek.

'I guess I need more help to flush him out,' he mused, then turned to Dalton. 'You want to return with me to Yellow Creek?'

'No, I ain't heading that way.'

'Then I could circle round and get you closer to where you are heading.'

Dalton glanced over his shoulder at the surrounding stark hills, imagining his chances of staying hidden from Vaughn without water, food, money, a horse, or a gun, then smiled.

'All right, I guess Yellow Creek is as good a destination as any.'

The sun was at its highest when Dalton and Sheriff Quentin rode into Yellow Creek.

Five years ago, the railroad had arrived. Since then, the town had moved beyond that first burst of expansion and had gained a confidence in itself. Freight wagons swirled the dust in this bustling town, but the well-stocked stores implied to Dalton that Yellow Creek now dreamt of achieving something.

Outside the sheriff's office, Dalton dismounted and bade his goodbyes, but he dawdled on the boardwalk until the sheriff had entered the office so that he could examine the Wanted posters on the notice board.

Unfortunately, one poster was all too clear.

WANTED: DALTON it said, and underneath that stark demand, there was a scrawled picture of a desperate man that could be pretty much anyone, followed by the phrase: For the murder of Sheriff Walker Dodge.

The poster provided no more details, but even if it had, a few words could never summarize Dalton's true crime. He'd killed a worthless and violent man to save other, decent folk, but however worthless that man was, Dalton was now a wanted man.

He'd hoped that by crossing the state line into Utah he could avoid too many details following him. But Walker Dodge's deputy was determined to follow him anywhere, and now this poster confirmed that for a man who'd killed a lawman, there could be no peace.

As he had been heading west and Yellow Creek backtracked from the place where he'd left Vaughn, Dalton reckoned the lawman wouldn't assume he'd headed here. And that meant he had some time before Vaughn arrived looking for him.

But not much.

Dalton sighed and glanced up and down the road, looking for any place where he could earn enough for a quick passage out of town. With so much bustle and trade, the opportunities for any man who had two strong hands and a desire to work were great.

But on seeing the Hotel Splendour, and remembering Stirling's suggestion, he headed there for his first attempt.

Inside, the reception room was clean and well-scrubbed, lacking the broken furniture and stench of rot that had permeated the few hotels Dalton had ever paid to enter.

Dalton tipped his hat to the bellboy in a neat red uniform who held the door open for him. This young man appraised Dalton's lack of luggage and his threadbare and dust-coated clothing, but then provided a hopeful smile and an outstretched and cupped hand.

Dalton returned a wink, then turned to the reception desk, where the portly receptionist was also considering Dalton's downtrodden state with a sneering curl to his lip. But as Dalton approached the desk, he replaced it with an ingratiating smile.

'I'm Wallace Falstein, the owner of the Hotel Splendour,' he said, then raised his eyebrows as he placed a pen on his open reception book.

Dalton swung to a halt before the desk.

'And I'm Da . . .' Dalton took a deep breath. 'Dave.'

'Well, Dave. Rooms are a dollar a night. Can you afford that?'

'Nope. But I don't want no room. I'm looking for work and I'd heard you're looking for someone.'

Wallace firmed his jaw, then waved in the general direction of the door in a bored manner that suggested he'd already suffered this question too many times today.

'I had a position, but filled it this morning.'

Dalton flashed a smile. 'Any chance of another job coming up any time soon?'

Wallace chuckled a harsh snort. 'Not unless Stirling Kimball roars through town again and shoots up another bellboy.'

'You had a position because . . .' Dalton winced, then turned to the door. 'Obliged for your time.'

With his head down, he wandered across the reception room, but the bellboy paced out to stand before him.

'So, you're looking for work, are you?' he said. When Dalton nodded, he drew him aside with a conspiratorial hand. 'If you're desperate, you can sit outside. One stage a day stops here, and one's due within the hour.'

'And do what?'

'People who stay at our hotel tip for having their bags carried inside.' The bellboy grined and waggled his eyebrows. 'Then they tip for having them carried to their rooms. So make sure you direct them to Ryan Foxglove.'

'And why don't you do both, Ryan, and earn twice the tips?'

Ryan glanced at Wallace, then lowered his voice, his flat tone suggesting he was quoting.

'It ain't – sorry, isn't – becoming for the staff of the Hotel Splendour to loiter on the road.'

'I can see that. But it don't sound like much in the way of work to me.'

Ryan leaned towards him. 'It isn't, but I've done it for the last month. Then I got lucky last night. Stirling Kimball shot Saul Merrill, and I was in just the right position to get a better job.'

'I'm pleased for you.' Dalton glanced outside, frowning, but then turned back. 'Did you earn much?'

'Enough to eat, sometimes.' Ryan shrugged. 'Like I said, you can sit outside if you're desperate.'

Dalton patted Ryan's shoulder then headed outside. On the boardwalk, he appraised the relative merits of working somewhere where he was hidden from casual view against being on the road and so being in a position where he could see Vaughn when he arrived.

He shrugged, then leaned back against the hotel wall and, with the hot sun blasting against that wall, slid his back down to the ground. From under a lowered hat, he watched the townsfolk come and go.

An hour into the afternoon, Dalton detected a strengthening in the bustle on the road. Storekeepers emerged to peer along the road, people loitered with more intent, and everyone glanced around.

Dalton stood, batted as much of the dust from his clothes as he could and stood on the edge of the boardwalk. He aped Wallace's ingratiating smile and peered down the road.

Sure enough, the stagecoach arrived, dust billowing behind, along with a trail of onlookers. The driver swung the stage in towards the hotel using a wide arc, then pulled back, holding the reins high. His boot slammed the brake lever and, with much creaking and hollering, the three-team stage drew to a halt outside the hotel.

Through the stage window, Dalton saw that only two men were within.

The first man alighted. He was squat and surly. His deep-set eyes appraised Dalton, then the length of the boardwalk. He rolled his shoulders, then turned and nodded to the second man, who alighted.

Dalton's gaze caught on the expensive cut of this man's suit, and even more on the leather suitcases that the driver lowered from the roof. On each case, the gold-embossed name RAPHAEL HUFFMAN stood out. But the first man, on seeing Dalton's interest, swung his jacket aside to reveal a shining Colt Peacemaker.

Dalton coughed and backed a pace to the wall.

'That was a fine journey,' Raphael announced as he shook the driver's hand.

A smile emerged on the driver's face as a bill changed hands.

'Anything to oblige a gentleman such as yourself,' he said, tipping his hat.

Raphael turned to Dalton, his clean brow furrowed.

'And why are my cases still sitting in the dirt?' he asked, his eyebrows raised.

'No reason,' Dalton said.

'Then move them. Come on, Boyd. We have much to do.'

The other man, Boyd, glared at Dalton, then filed in before Raphael, and the two men headed through the opened door. Inside, Ryan stood to the side with his head bowed and his cupped left hand protruding.

Dalton grabbed the smallest case, thrust it under his arm, then thrust the next smallest under his other arm. He wrestled the two larger cases into each hand, then followed them into the hotel.

Ryan kept a heel back, holding the door open

and, as Dalton staggered in, Raphael shook Ryan's hand. A smile emerged on Ryan's face as Raphael whispered something to him. Then Raphael marched to the reception desk.

Ryan winked at Dalton, then scurried across the reception room and into a side-room.

'Mr Huffman,' Wallace said, beaming and holding his hat high, 'we didn't expect you until tomorrow. Not that we're not delighted you're here early.'

'Of course not,' Raphael said, standing before the desk and lifting up and down on his heels. 'But it's been a long journey and I'll be in my usual – room sixteen. Boyd will take room seventeen.'

Wallace gulped, his eyes flashing with a hint of something, perhaps irritation, before he placed the reception book before Raphael and swivelled it round.

'And would you mind signing the book while we have you installed?'

As Raphael leaned over the book, Dalton headed for the stairs.

Wallace pointed out the right place for Raphael to write, then scurried out from behind the reception desk and grabbed Dalton's arm, halting him.

'I'm sorry I'm in your hotel again,' Dalton said. 'But Ryan's just gone and I'm—'

'Don't worry about that.' Wallace led Dalton to the bottom of the stairs and lowered his voice. 'Here's the key. Go . . .' Wallace glanced at Dalton's full hands, but Dalton opened his mouth and Wallace prised the key into the corner of his mouth. 'Go to room sixteen and throw any clothes you find in there out into the corridor. If they're all gone by the time Raphael arrives, you'll get fifty cents.'

'And,' Dalton said from the corner of his mouth, 'what if the owner of the clothes is in the room?'

'Then you get a dollar.'

Dalton nodded and strode up the stairs, two at a time, then bustled down the corridor to room sixteen. He dropped the cases at his feet, thrust the key in the lock, finding that it was unlocked, then threw open the door.

Inside, a man was sitting by the window, staring at the boots he'd placed on a writing-desk.

'Ah,' he said, 'I ordered room service an hour ago. My boots need clean—'

'They don't,' Dalton muttered. 'Get your boots on and get our hide out of here.'

'I am Julian Carter.' He folded his arms and puffed his chest. 'And I am not going anywhere.'

Dalton swung Raphael's cases into the room, then rolled his shoulders and paced towards Julian, one steady pace at a time.

'Mighty pleased to meet you, Julian. Now, *go*.'

'I will not.'

Dalton strode past Julian and grabbed the boots from the writing-desk, then dragged the window open.

'Then I'll throw your boots out the window.' He faced Julian and smiled. 'And then, you'll follow them.'

As Julian gulped, then scurried to the door, Dalton

turned to the wardrobe. He grabbed the clothes from inside then back-kicked the door closed, but as Julian was still loitering in the doorway, he slapped them into Julian's chest, swung him round, and marched him into the corridor.

'I . . . I really must protest,' Julian whined, digging his heels in and forcing Dalton to shove him out. 'I paid for this room for another day.'

Boyd's heavy footfalls were pacing up the stairs.

'But Wallace said a fine patron like you deserved a better room. He's put you in room twenty-four.'

'And about time, too,' Julian said. He shrugged from Dalton's grip, then strode off down the corridor, but Dalton was already dashing back into room sixteen.

He transferred Raphael's cases to the bed, then smoothed the blankets. He glanced around the room, searching for other signs of Julian's habitation, then saw the boots on the writing-desk. With a shrug he hurled them through the open window.

Even before the boots had hit the ground, Boyd was striding in, leaving Raphael standing in the corridor. He sneered at Dalton, then stalked around the room, glaring into each corner, and rattled the door to the adjoining room seventeen. He nodded and beckoned Raphael to enter, but Raphael stopped two paces in from the door and sniffed.

'This room smells,' he said.

'I thought so, too,' Dalton said, wrinkling his nose and peering around. 'So, I opened the window.'

'Good man, good man.' Raphael headed to the

writing-desk by the window, drew a pen, then scrawled on a sheet of paper. 'Fetch these items and don't take long about it.'

Dalton took the list, finding that Raphael had placed two bills behind it without him noticing. He nodded and headed outside, but it was only to walk straight into Julian, who pointed back down the corridor.

'There is no room twenty-four,' he whined.

Dalton glanced down the corridor, seeing a door ajar, two doors away. So, he pushed him towards that door.

'My mistake. Wallace must have meant *that* room is now ready for you.' Julian wandered towards the open door. 'I guess it won't hurt to look.'

Dalton waited, ensuring that Julian didn't emerge, and discovered that Raphael had given him a ten-dollar and one-dollar bill. He tucked the one-dollar bill into his top pocket and, when the door to Julian's new room closed, dashed down the stairs to the reception desk.

Around the desk, Wallace was barking orders to what looked like the hotel's entire staff complement. As each order ended, the ordered person scurried off in a different direction. Dalton fought a path to Wallace's side and held out the list.

'I'll pay you later,' Wallace said, not even looking at the list.

'But I got a list of things Raphael needs.'

The remaining staff uttered a collective sigh.

'Dave, nobody has the time.' Wallace kneaded his

brow. 'We all have things to get that Mr Huffman needs. Just do it yourself.'

'But I don't work for . . .'

Ryan edged through the milling people and slapped a hand on Dalton's arm, then drew him aside.

'You're right. You don't work here,' he said, then snorted. 'But for a desperate man, you aren't thinking straight. If Mr Huffman wants something, it's profitable to just get it.'

Dalton glanced at the bill in his hand and smiled.

'I guess I can see that.'

Raphael's requirements were easy to find. He wanted a change of clothes, paper, ink, and the most recent newspapers available.

With Ryan's help, Dalton located the appropriate stores and, within fifteen minutes, returned to the hotel. In the reception room, a sleepy atmosphere had replaced the confusion that had reigned when Dalton had left, but as Dalton passed the reception desk, Wallace mimed wiping sweat from his brow.

Dalton headed up to Raphael's room, knocked, and to a gruff request to enter, wandered in.

Raphael was hunched over his writing-desk. Ryan was hanging clothes in the wardrobe. The door to the adjoining room seventeen was open and Boyd stood in the doorway watching Ryan's every movement with his upper lip curled in his apparently permanent distrust.

Dalton passed Ryan the new clothes, then placed

the paper, ink and newspaper on the edge of the writing-desk. He rummaged in his pocket for the change, taking an inordinate amount of time to locate every last coin, but Raphael delivered a disdainful shake of the head, and Dalton dropped the money back into his pocket.

Raphael grunted his appreciation of the quality of the paper and ink that Dalton had purchased, then leaned back to throw the newspaper on to the bed behind him.

Dalton rose and lowered on his heels, but as neither new orders nor a final tip appeared, he turned to the door. Behind him, Ryan closed the wardrobe and followed him.

'Read me the front page, Ryan,' Raphael said, not looking up from his writing-desk.

'What front page?' Ryan said, his voice high-pitched.

'The front page of the newspaper. Read it to me.'

Ryan glanced at the newspaper then, with his brow furrowed, shuffled it open.

'Don't you want to read it yourself?' he said with a pronounced gulp.

'If I had time to do that, I wouldn't ask you to read it. And I can hardly ask Boyd.'

As Boyd grunted, Ryan turned the newspaper and peered at it, but from the door, Dalton saw that he was holding it upside-down.

'Ryan, you'd better go,' he said. 'Wallace needs you urgently. I'll read to Raphael.'

Ryan flashed Dalton a relieved smile, then passed

him the newspaper and hurried by. When Ryan closed the door, Dalton looked up to see that Raphael had turned in his seat and was looking at him with a sly smile on his face.

'I can see you will be a very useful man, Dave, very useful indeed.'

Dalton smiled, but as he raised the newspaper, he saw that Boyd had now turned the full glare of his distrusting gaze on him.

CHAPTER 4

'Obliged for your help earlier,' Ryan said as he joined Dalton by the hotel door.

'You helped me,' Dalton said, watching Boyd lead Raphael into the dining-room. 'And one good deed leads to another. At least, most of the time.'

'In that case, are you coming to the kitchen to eat?'

Dalton held his hands wide, directing Ryan's gaze to his threadbare clothes.

'I don't work here.' With his new status as Raphael's main helper, Wallace had let him stand inside the hotel, although, to Dalton's relief, he hadn't tried to make him wear a uniform.

'Perhaps not, but I reckon that any man who is useful to Mr Huffman can eat leftovers in the kitchen.'

Dalton's stomach grumbled, but he shook his head.

'I'll wait until after Raphael's eaten.'

Ryan jingled the change in his pocket.

'You're learning.'

'Hey, bellboy.' The demand came from the dining-room door.

Both Dalton and Ryan swung round, but the man who emerged from the dining-room was only Boyd and he was striding towards Dalton.

Ryan wavered a moment, then headed into the kitchen.

'Does Raphael want me?' Dalton asked, pushing himself from the wall.

'Can't see anyone wanting the likes of you.' Boyd swung to a halt before Dalton. He edged his jacket aside, letting Dalton see his Peacemaker, then placed his hands on his hips and looked Dalton up and down. 'But you must be right desperate if you're hoping that Mr Huffman will throw you another scrap.'

With his teeth gritted, Dalton smiled.

'I guess I am. But I'm helping him. And that's all you should care about.'

'You're wrong. I reckon you're getting too close to him. You've had your tips. Now, stay away.'

'What's it to you who helps Raphael?'

Boyd turned to watch a servant scurry from the kitchen and into the dining-room, a plate of steaming stew held aloft, his head down.

'Everyone else here is as meek as a hotel worker should be. But you ain't like them. You looked Mr Huffman in the eye as if you reckoned you're his equal. And when someone with that attitude sniffs around Mr Huffman, I get worried.'

Dalton held his hands wide and placed a huge smile on his lips, but Boyd favoured Dalton with one last glare, then turned on his heel and strode back into the dining-room.

Dalton glanced at the reception desk, but although Wallace was standing behind the desk and, from his quick flinching back, had been listening to this conversation, Wallace now studiously avoided looking at him. Dalton edged back a pace, intending to lean against the wall again, but another demanding hunger pain rumbled deep in his guts.

So, with a shrug, he went to the kitchen.

There, a hodgepodge of scraps was available, but as Dalton hadn't eaten that day, he helped himself with relish.

In between mouthfuls, Ryan suggested that the alley outside the kitchen was a warm place to sleep. Apparently, for the last month he'd slept there, but after Saul Merrill's murder, his elevated status let him sleep in the cellar.

After eating, Dalton considered retiring to the alley, but in case any new patrons arrived, who needed bags carrying, he stood by the front door instead.

He waited for an hour. No new patrons did arrive, but Raphael did emerge from the dining-room, patting his stomach, a huge cigar held aloft. He nodded to Dalton, and Dalton tipped his hat, but Boyd returned a glare as Dalton opened the door for them.

Although Dalton didn't expect that Vaughn would

have arrived in Yellow Creek by now, he still glanced along the road, searching every shadowed length of boardwalk, then followed them, keeping around thirty yards back.

On the boardwalk, he watched Raphael and Boyd wander across the road to the nearest saloon, the Lucky Star. With a last glance along the road, Dalton followed them, but he stopped outside and peered through the window.

Inside, Boyd was clearing a path to the back wall by the simple expedient of pushing anyone who was foolish enough to loiter before him to the side. The pushed people returned a quick glare, but a variety of oaths from Boyd convinced them that they shouldn't complain.

With the path clear, Raphael joined Boyd then selected a table. Boyd ensured that it emptied. Then Boyd fetched Raphael a drink and stood over him, ensuring nobody got too close.

Having confirmed that Boyd never let Raphael leave his sight, and that the opportunities for Raphael to find him useful were limited, Dalton turned from the window.

A hand slapped on his shoulder. Dalton swirled round, his fists rising, but it was only Ryan.

'You heading in there?' Ryan asked, smiling hopefully.

'No.' Dalton lowered his fists.

'You're jumpy. Anyone would think you were a wanted man.'

'Yeah,' Dalton murmured, then stood tall. 'But

seeing as I ain't and you helped me get employment, I'll stand you a drink.'

Side by side, they strode inside. Dalton ordered whiskeys for both of them. Ryan gulped his down, but Dalton nursed his, ensuring that he didn't waste his limited funds as he waited for a polite amount of time to pass before he could leave this public place. But when he'd finished his drink, Ryan ordered more drinks.

Dalton objected, but Ryan raised a hand.

'You aren't paying again. You aren't the only one gaining now that Mr Huffman is in town.'

Dalton nodded, then leaned on the bar beside Ryan.

'He tipped you well, too?'

Ryan patted his pocket. 'Yep. Mr Huffman wanted me to find him a poker game, which I did.'

Dalton glanced over Ryan's shoulder. By the back wall, Raphael was holding court to a loud group of poker-players, regaling them with a tale, but Dalton wasn't close enough to hear it.

'You not got the funds to join yourself?'

Ryan spluttered over his drink, then shook his head.

'I don't reckon I'll ever play poker again – not after last night.'

'What happened last night?'

'Stirling Kimball, that's what happened.'

Dalton nodded. 'You mean Stirling shot Saul Merrill in a poker game?'

'Yeah. Stirling was staying in the hotel. He wanted

a game and, as he was clearly wealthier than everyone else in the hotel, we were glad to oblige him.'

'And he was a bad loser?'

'Not at first. He had one of the worst streaks of luck I've ever seen. He started losing and just couldn't stop. But then came a big hand. Me, Saul and Stirling all stayed in, but when Saul laid down his cards, Stirling just leapt at him. Before we knew what was happening, Saul was dead and Stirling was high-tailing it out of town.'

'Couldn't you do anything?'

Ryan raised his glass and swirled the whiskey.

'I'm not proud of myself, but when a man like Stirling draws his gun, you get out of the way any way you can and worry about everyone else later.'

'I can see that. And at least you got a better job.'

'Yeah, but I lost my enjoyment of Yellow Creek last night. I'll move on soon.'

'Me, too. I just want to earn enough to leave.' From the corner of the room, a loud peal of laughter ripped out. 'And from the sound of things, our bene-factor is enjoying himself.'

'He's just making himself popular now that he's buying into Yellow Creek. Everyone reckons he'll be the biggest businessman in town come the fall.'

'I wondered why he needed Boyd at his side. That man seems mighty . . .' From the corner of his eye, Dalton saw Boyd striding towards the bar.

'Mighty what?'

'Mighty close to us.'

'Dave,' Boyd muttered, stomping to a halt behind

Dalton and Ryan, 'you just don't listen, do you?'

Dalton turned. 'Howdy, Boyd. We're just enjoying a quiet drink.'

'You ain't. You're sniffing around, hoping to please Mr Huffman again. But this ain't the only saloon in town.' Boyd rolled his shoulders and thrust his face forwards. 'So, scat!'

Dalton glanced to the side. The group of men beside him had stopped their conversation to watch what he did next, but he just reached behind hin and grabbed his drink, then slowly lifted it to his lips. He downed his whiskey, still keeping his gaze on Boyd.

'Obliged for the advice.' He reached back and placed the glass on the bar behind him, then tipped his hat. 'I'll drink somewhere else.'

'Hey,' Ryan said, slapping an arm across Dalton's chest and stopping him from turning to the door. 'He can't tell us where to drink.'

'And he ain't,' Dalton said. 'I'm just choosing to go.'

Ryan stepped back from Dalton, sneering. 'Then go. I'm not drinking with someone who takes orders from a man like this.'

As Boyd grunted his irritation, Dalton turned his back on him.

'Ryan,' Dalton said, 'I know you're feeling guilty about last night, but picking a fight ain't wise.'

Ryan looked Dalton up and down, snorted, then leaned over the bar, turning his back on him.

Dalton watched Boyd lick his lips, then file in beside Ryan to order drinks from the bartender. The group of men standing at the bar muttered their poor opinion of Dalton's attitude, but Dalton still left the saloon.

On the other side of the road, he stopped and, in the shadows, watched the saloon.

For the next hour, he kept his silent vigil, in between looking for any newcomers arriving in town.

Then Ryan wandered out and headed down the road in the opposite direction to the hotel.

A minute later, Boyd emerged and followed Ryan.

Dalton pushed himself from the wall and followed them, staying about twenty yards back from Boyd.

With his arms swinging and his gait casual, Ryan walked towards the next saloon on the road, but just as he paced off the boardwalk to cross the road, Boyd hailed him, making Ryan turn.

On seeing Boyd, Ryan flinched and backed away a pace, but Boyd dashed three long paces and grabbed Ryan's collar, then dragged him into the alley beside the bank.

Several people were walking nearby and, from so close by, they must have seen Boyd's action, but they turned away and hurried past the alley.

Dalton broke into a run and dashed down the road. He reached the alley ten seconds after Boyd had dragged Ryan into it. Inside, Boyd had slammed Ryan against the wall, the slash of light and darkness from the bank wall cutting across them.

Ryan squirmed, trying to break Boyd's hold of him, but Boyd pulled Ryan higher so that he had to stand on tiptoe. He grunted an oath, then slugged

Ryan deep in the guts and released him. Ryan folded over the blow and staggered back into the darkness of the alley, spitting bile.

As Boyd raised a fist and stood over Ryan, waiting for him to right himself so that he could punch him again, Dalton paced into the alley.

'Hey,' he muttered, 'stop that!'

Boyd flinched then swirled round from Ryan to face Dalton.

'Go away,' he grunted, 'yellow-belly.'

'I ain't no yellow-belly. And I ain't going away.'

Boyd licked his lips and grinned as he paced down the alley towards Dalton.

'Now that sure is good news.' Boyd ripped his gun from its holster and turned it on Dalton. 'But I reckon I'll still punch some holes in you and see what colour your insides are.'

Dalton raised his hands as behind Boyd, Ryan rolled to his feet and shuffled down the alley, his fists raised and ready to jump Boyd. But Dalton directed a shake of his head towards him, making Ryan halt.

'You got no reason to shoot me,' Dalton said, his voice low. 'Neither Ryan nor me are a threat to Raphael.'

Boyd snorted. Then his shoulders slumped and he twirled his gun into his holster. He took a step towards Dalton, then swung around to kick Ryan's feet from under him, bundling him to the ground. Then he stalked from the alley, but he stopped beside Dalton.

'It ain't about that no more,' he said, looking into

40

the road. 'Now, you don't just stay away from Mr Huffman. You stay away from me, too.'

From the corner of his eye, Boyd glanced at Dalton, his gaze cold and sneering, then turned and swaggered back down the road towards the Lucky Star saloon.

Dalton watched until he sure Boyd was leaving them, then hunkered down beside Ryan.

'You fine?' he asked, pulling Ryan to a sitting position.

'Yeah,' Ryan muttered, rubbing his guts. 'I guess.'

'Did Boyd reckon you'd faced him down in the saloon?'

'He didn't say nothing about that. He just reckoned I was getting too close to Mr Huffman.'

Dalton sighed. 'I had the same problem with him earlier. That's why I left the saloon.'

'I can see that now.' Ryan rubbed the back of his head. 'But I'm glad you're here. You didn't seem the kind of man who'd avoid a fight.'

'And I ain't. I just have to be careful.'

'Have to?' Ryan asked, standing.

'That ain't important.' Dalton set his hands on his hips. 'But now that Boyd's pushed this beyond a threat, what are we doing about him?'

'I don't rightly know. Mr Huffman's hired Boyd to protect him, and he's doing that. I guess now we *should* stay out of his way. The tips aren't worth that much.'

Dalton glanced up and down the road, then followed Ryan out of the alley.

'Trouble is,' he said to himself, 'I got no choice.'

'I didn't expect to see you again,' Sheriff Quentin said, looking up from his desk.

Dalton wandered through the door and into the sheriff's office.

'I'll be in town for a while,' he said, 'now that I'm working in the Hotel Splendour. So, I wanted to check that you're not bearing a grudge against me no more.'

'I ain't. You made an honest mistake.' Quentin sighed. 'But that don't stop me wishing you hadn't made it. And if you're here to give me information as to where Stirling Kimball is, I'll feel even more forgiving towards you.'

'I don't have information on him.' Dalton paced across the room to stand before Quentin's desk. 'But I do have information on another troublemaker – Boyd Dooley, Raphael Huffman's hired gun.'

Quentin jutted his jaw, nodding. 'I've heard that Raphael's man takes his duties seriously, but that he doesn't overstep those duties.'

'But he's already done that. Boyd beat somebody up tonight.'

'That *somebody* want to press charges?'

Dalton frowned. 'Nope.'

Quentin shrugged. 'Then I can't do nothing.'

'I know. But I'm just suggesting that you watch him. Raphael is in a poker game in the Lucky Star saloon, and I reckon that no matter who wins, Boyd will take exception to another *somebody* before the night is over.'

'I hear what you're saying. Obliged for the information, Dave.'

Dalton turned to the door, but then glanced over his shoulder.

'I never gave you my name.'

From under a lowered hat, Quentin peered up at Dalton.

'You didn't.'

Dalton returned Quentin's gaze, then left the office and headed back to his former position facing the Lucky Star saloon.

Ten minutes later, Sheriff Quentin wandered outside and down the road to the saloon.

From his position, Dalton watched Quentin through the window, drinking at the bar. But, from time to time, Quentin glanced over his shoulder and towards the poker game in the corner of the saloon.

At least an hour had passed when a barked demand ripped out from the saloon.

Quentin swung round from the bar, but then tables and chairs scraped back and several people surged out in to the road, blocking Dalton's view of what Quentin did next.

A gunshot blasted. Urgent orders ripped out.

More people crowded into the doorway and spilled out on to the road, but then they parted and Quentin stormed through the batwings, holding Boyd in a firm arm-lock from behind, and marched him down the road.

Raphael dashed out after them and hailed Quentin, forcing Quentin to stop, but after a short, grunted disagreement, Quentin escorted Boyd to his office, leaving Raphael standing on the boardwalk with his hands on his hips.

Dalton waited until Raphael strode off the boardwalk and headed towards the hotel, then took a diagonal route across the road that cut across his journey.

'Raphael,' he hailed, 'what's happened?'

In the middle of the road, Raphael stopped and turned to Dalton, frowning.

'I was just in a right friendly poker game. Then the sheriff took exception to Boyd doing his job.'

Dalton shrugged. 'Boyd not fire that gunshot, then?'

'He did, but that's no reason to go and arrest a man.'

'Perhaps Quentin reckoned Boyd can be too keen sometimes.'

'To my way of thinking, Boyd couldn't be *too* keen.'

'You may be right.' Dalton rubbed his chin, then set his hands on his hips in a deliberate aping of Boyd's belligerent posture. 'But being as Boyd might be in a cell for a while, do you need help?'

CHAPTER 5

'Do you know what I'm doing?' Raphael asked as he crossed the road.

'Nope,' Dalton said. 'But you need protection. And I'm offering my services.'

Raphael nodded as he stopped on the boardwalk outside the Hotel Splendour.

'And perhaps you can help.' Raphael folded his arms. 'I am setting up a business deal in which substantial amounts of cash will change hands. Does that worry you?'

'Nope.' Dalton smiled. 'And the pay?'

'Fifty dollars if the deal goes smoothly. Nothing if it doesn't.' Raphael turned to glance down the road. 'So, for tonight, look around town. Locate the troublemakers. Ensure they aren't a threat to me.'

Dalton shuffled from foot to foot, then held his threadbare jacket wide.

'I can do that, and I guess you can see that I'm

desperate, but even so, I won't get involved in anything that ain't legal.'

A momentary smile trembled Raphael's lips before he masked it by rubbing his jaw.

'Understood. But you have nothing to worry about.' Raphael waved his hands at full stretch, then pointed up at the hotel. 'Because in two days, I am buying the Hotel Splendour.'

Dalton nodded, but Raphael didn't look at him as he turned and headed into the hotel. Dalton glanced along the road, then walked down the boardwalk towards the Lucky Star saloon.

'Now,' a voice drawled from the shadows, 'that was right interesting.'

Dalton flinched, but the man who emerged from the alley wasn't Vaughn. Neither was any of the four men standing behind him. Dalton narrowed his eyes and reckoned that these men were probably the men who had been drinking beside him and Ryan earlier.

'Why?' Dalton said.

'The name's Hunter.' He gestured to the side. 'And this is Gus and—'

'And I ain't interested in your names.'

Hunter glanced at the other men, his bottom lip pouting with mock hurt.

'And there was me being all friendly. But it seems you just ain't a friendly sort of man.'

'If you want to say something, say it, otherwise, I am a busy man.'

Dalton moved to head down the boardwalk, but

the men spread out, blocking his route.

'I do have something to say. Earlier, you avoided a fight with Boyd Dooley in the saloon. Then, you got Boyd arrested. Now, you have Boyd's job.' Hunter licked his lips and smirked. 'So, yeah, you have had a busy day.'

'I sure have. And it ain't finished.'

Dalton slapped a hand on Hunter's shoulder and pushed, but Hunter set his legs wide and resisted his attempt to barge him aside.

Hunter sniggered with a lively grin on his face, but when Dalton removed his hand and squared up to him, he tipped his hat and stood aside.

Dalton glanced at the other men, all of whom grinned, then backed away. So, Dalton paced down the boardwalk towards the saloon, but although he could hear Hunter and the others chortling behind him, he didn't look back.

As Raphael's new hired gun, Dalton got to sleep in Boyd's former room.

Aside from accompanying Raphael whenever he left his room, and ensuring nobody got too close, his duties weren't onerous.

First thing in the morning, he ensured that Raphael's breakfast exactly met his instructions: one thick slice of bread, lightly buttered, and one glass of milk.

Then he headed into town to buy more fresh paper and to locate copies of every newspaper he could find.

The fact that some were copies of the same news-paper didn't concern Raphael. And, with the promise of fifty dollars for less than two days of work, Dalton decided not to risk his employment by asking why.

He figured that when Raphael closed his deal he would have sufficient funds to leave town, then lie low for a while.

And when Raphael announced that he had a busi-ness trip to make out of town, he even bought Dalton a horse, a gun, and a complete change of clothing.

Even better, nothing in his demeanour suggested that these wouldn't be his permanent possessions.

In late afternoon, they rode out of Yellow Creek and headed west.

As Dalton had been westward bound when Vaughn had ambushed him, he held his head high and darted his gaze between every likely source of an ambush. Luckily, Raphael took this diligent obser-vance as being a sign of his new duties.

'What is the most money you have ever seen, Dave?' Raphael asked when they were ten miles out of town.

'A hundred dollars.' Dalton shrugged. 'Perhaps less.'

'I thought so. I am meeting my business partner for him to give me his share of our investment.' Raphael reached back and unhooked a carpet-bag from his saddle, then threw it to Dalton. 'You will then have eight hundred dollars in this saddlebag in cash. Does that concern you?'

'Nope.' Dalton hefted the bag, then firmed his jaw. 'I'll ensure nobody steals it.'

'And I'm sure that is good news for any . . . any prospective thieves.' Dalton swung round in the saddle to face Raphael.

'What you mean?'

'I mean that my business partner has a temper, and any thief who was foolhardy enough to steal that cash would face a shortened life. So, you will do any thief a service by ensuring that he doesn't take the money.'

'Perhaps if your business partner is so concerned about his money, he should protect it himself.'

'He has . . . he has reasons for staying out of town and letting me complete the deal.'

Dalton shrugged and, with that, they returned to riding quietly.

Another mile down the trail, they veered off and rode along an old, overgrown track.

A mile off the trail, they approached a massive outcropping of rock. Only a horse tethered to a Joshua tree suggested that anyone had been here in years.

Fifty yards from the rock, Raphael dismounted. He took the carpet-bag from Dalton, but when Dalton moved to dismount, he shook his head and ordered him to keep guard.

Dalton nodded and turned his horse to peer down the track, leaving Raphael to head around the rock.

He ran his gaze along the distant hills, but aside

from the occasional swooping buzzard, saw no movement.

Raphael's horse and his business partner's horse stood side by side, rooting for nourishment in the dirt, and this encouraged his own horse to edge towards them. With no sign of trouble nearby, Dalton let it mooch forward.

The horse that had been here when he arrived caught his eye or, more particularly, he noticed the blanket protruding from under the saddlebag. It was red, the same colour as the one he'd owned before Stirling Kimball stole it.

Dalton shook his head, dismissing the fanciful thought, but as he looked at the blanket, he noticed a frayed edge of cloth, again as frayed as his blanket had been.

So, with his brow furrowed, he dismounted.

He edged to the horse and lifted a corner of the blanket. He'd purchased a common one, but still, he couldn't shake the thought that this was his blanket.

Even though the horse wasn't his, he wandered towards the rock, but he continued to peer around so that he could claim he was scouting around if Raphael emerged.

He climbed up thirty yards of scree until he reached the point where the rock became vertical, then edged around until Raphael came into view.

Raphael and his business partner were about fifty yards away, chatting with their backs to him, their light tones easy and familiar, even though Dalton couldn't make out the words. The rock's shadow shrouded each man.

But despite the shadow, Dalton recognized Raphael's business partner.

He was Stirling Kimball.

CHAPTER 6

'You're quiet, Dave,' Raphael said when they were a mile down the trail, heading back towards Yellow Creek.

Dalton glanced over his shoulder, confirming that Stirling wasn't following them, but then leaned back to pat his saddlebag to cover his action.

'Just looking out for trouble.'

'And do we have trouble now?' Raphael glanced at Dalton. 'You're looking over your shoulder as much as forwards. You reckon that someone's following us?'

'No. It's just . . .' Dalton took a deep breath. 'If I'm to ensure you avoid trouble, I should have checked that your meeting-place was secure first.'

Raphael smiled. 'You *are* taking your duties seriously.'

'I am. Boyd searched out trouble then dealt with it. I prefer to avoid trouble happening in the first place.'

'That is a good policy.' Raphael leaned forward

and stared straight ahead, then shrugged and lowered his voice. 'But as you ignored my orders and saw my business partner, what are you now thinking?'

From the corner of his eye, Dalton glanced at Raphael, judging how an honest answer might affect him, but saw nothing in his inscrutable profile to suggest what his response would be.

'I'm worried,' he said, his voice guarded. 'Stirling Kimball is a wanted man.'

'Don't judge a man you don't know. That fact pains him more than it worries you, but nothing must halt this deal. Once it is complete, I hope he'll turn himself in and explain everything.'

'I hope so, too.'

For a full minute Raphael rode in silence, then turned to Dalton.

'And that means you don't need to see Sheriff Quentin.' Raphael raised his eyebrows. 'Like you did with Boyd.'

Dalton bit his bottom lip, but couldn't stop himself wincing.

'I only saw Quentin to report that Boyd had beaten Ryan.'

'And I'm sure that was an honourable reason.' Raphael turned in the saddle to face ahead. 'But don't give me cause to think you had another motive.'

An hour before sundown, Dalton and Raphael arrived back in Yellow Creek. While Raphael headed into the hotel, Dalton went straight into the bank and deposited the bag of cash.

The teller was expecting him and counted the money efficiently, the amount coming to exactly the total Raphael had promised – $800, which the teller added to Raphael's current balance of $1,315.

With the money safely deposited, Dalton glanced up and down the road, but he recognized the horses that stood outside the Lucky Star saloon as being the same ones that he'd seen last night. As Raphael planned to ponder the details of tomorrow's hotel sale and didn't need him for the rest of the evening, he headed into the saloon.

Ryan was already propping up the bar, so Dalton joined him and slapped his shoulder. Ryan flinched and swirled round to confront him, but then smiled on seeing that it was Dalton.

'Dave,' he murmured, 'don't sneak up on me like that.'

'You expecting trouble?'

'Yeah.' Ryan glanced at the saloon door, then wrung his hands. 'This afternoon Sheriff Quentin released Boyd Dooley.'

Dalton nodded. 'And has Boyd seen you?'

'Yeah. He waylaid me outside the Long Trail saloon. He didn't have a problem with me, but he does have a problem with you.'

'Then why are you so jumpy?'

'Because when a man like Boyd has a few drinks in him, he might forget that.'

Dalton sighed and leaned on the bar beside Ryan. 'Does he reckon I turned him in?'

Ryan nodded. 'I guess he did himself some think-ing in that cell.'

'Then it's a pity he chose today to do that for the first time.'

Ryan stared at Dalton, then joined him in laugh-ing.

Although both men frequently glanced at the door, they settled in for a pleasant evening.

Two hours after sundown, the room was bustling when Dalton ordered another drink, but Ryan slapped Dalton in the stomach before he'd attracted the bartender's attention.

'Boyd's here,' he said, then hunched over the bar.

Dalton matched Ryan's posture and listened to the firm footfalls pace across the room until Boyd stood beside him. Dalton placed a large smile on his face, then rolled his head to the side.

'Howdy, Boyd,' he said, 'you want a drink?'

'You got some nerve asking me that after you took my job.' Boyd slammed a fist on the bar, then grabbed Dalton's collar and dragged him round to face him. 'Two years working for that no-good varmint. Then I get into another fight and what happens? He doesn't want me and doesn't even pay me off.'

Dalton grabbed Boyd's hand and prised it from his collar, then pushed him back a pace.

'When Quentin arrested you, you weren't defend-ing Raphael.'

'Anybody that got too close was just plain trouble.'

Boyd rolled his shoulders, but Ryan paced to the

side to stand beside Dalton.

'But,' Ryan said, 'not everyone was looking for a beating.'

Boyd glanced at Ryan, then bunched his fists and squared up to Dalton, but when Dalton just sneered, Boyd hurled back his fist and threw a punch at Dalton's face.

Dalton ducked the punch and, with his head down, rushed Boyd, aiming to throw him on his back, but Boyd set his squat legs wide and resisted, then hurled Dalton back against the bar.

Boyd advanced, but Ryan leapt on his back, wrapped an arm around his neck, and tried to pull his head back. Boyd rolled his shoulders, then threw his head down, bundling Ryan over his shoulders to land him on the floor at his feet. He ripped back his foot, but before he could kick Ryan, Dalton hurled a wild punch at Boyd's head. It connected with solid force, but Boyd just shrugged off the blow, then kicked Ryan anyway.

Ryan folded over the blow, then rolled away, but it gave Dalton enough time to rip back his fist and crunch a blow into Boyd's chin. This time, Boyd's head cracked back and he tottered away from Dalton. But, with a rub of his chin, he regained his stance and appraised Dalton, then spat on his fist and stormed in.

Dalton danced back, Boyd's first blow whistling by his nose, but Boyd followed through with a left jab to the guts that blasted all the wind from Dalton's body. As Dalton staggered into a table, scattering glasses,

Boyd advanced on him, then thundered a blow into his cheek that sent Dalton wheeling over the table.

Dalton landed on his knees and dragged in great breaths, but Boyd dashed around the table, slammed firm hands on his back, and pulled him to his feet.

Still winded, Dalton had to force himself to raise his fists, but as Boyd hurled back his own fist, Ryan advanced on Boyd from behind and smashed a chair over his head. Splinters flew in all directions, but Boyd just shook his head then reached back, grabbed Ryan's collar, and pulled him round to face him.

He grinned as he stood Ryan straight then hurled a blow at Ryan's face that crashed him into a group of men sitting around a table. Ryan and the men collapsed in an entangled heap on the floor. Then Boyd turned, but it was only to walk into a crunching blow to the nose from Dalton, Ryan's intervention giving him the time to regain his breath.

Boyd staggered back, clutching his nose, but Dalton followed through with a flurry of blows. The first two landed with little effect, but the third knocked Boyd to the floor.

Dalton didn't give Boyd enough time to regain his footing; he pulled him to his feet then thundered a blow to his cheek that spun him into the bar. As Boyd collapsed over the bar, heaving great gasps of air, Dalton paced to his side, grabbed the back of his head, and slammed it on to the bartop.

Boyd threw a weak backhand at Dalton's chest, but Dalton slammed his forehead on the bar a second, and a third time. Only when Boyd uttered a pained bleat did Dalton release his grip and let him slump to the floor.

Dalton regained his breath, then dragged the limp Boyd to his feet. With a firm grip of his collar and belt, he marched him to the door and hurled him outside. As the batwings swung to a halt, he turned and headed to the bar, patting his hands together.

Ryan was righting himself and apologizing to everyone that he'd upended, but Dalton hailed the bartender.

'How much damage did we cause?' he asked.

'Not that much,' the bartender said. 'If Boyd doesn't drink in here no more, it'll be worth it.'

'Obliged that—'

'Dave,' Boyd roared, kicking back the batwings, his gun drawn and aimed at him, 'nobody does that to me.'

CHAPTER 7

Dalton turned and faced the gun-toting Boyd as, around the saloon, the customers scattered, leaving Dalton alone by the bar.

Ryan joined the other customers, but then slipped behind the onlookers, aiming to outflank Boyd.

Dalton edged to the bar to ensure that Ryan stayed out of Boyd's view.

'I have had enough of you,' Boyd grunted. 'You stole my job.'

'I didn't steal your job. I just got lucky when you lost it. But after tomorrow, I'll leave, and if you're lucky, Raphael might employ you again.'

Boyd snorted. 'If he does, he does. But either way, I want to see if you can use that gun Mr Huffman bought you.'

'Has everybody seen that I tried to avoid this?' Dalton shouted, glancing around the saloon. 'I got no desire to kill this man, but if he forces me, I will do it.'

Boyd's right eye twitched with the first hint of doubt that he could kill Dalton. He glanced at Dalton's gun, then at the hand that Dalton edged down to rest just above the holster with the fingers dangling.

'That was a weak boast. You won't kill me.'

'I won't if you leave.' Dalton rolled his shoulders and set his feet wide. 'But you can do that either head first like last time, or feet first.'

With his left hand, Boyd rubbed his mouth, the hand shaking for the first time. In a nervous gesture, he glanced over his shoulder at the door, but at that moment, Ryan leapt out from the onlookers and rushed Boyd.

Boyd flinched and swung round to face the advancing Ryan, but Ryan bundled into him, knocking his gun to the floor.

As Boyd and Ryan struggled, Dalton dashed across the room and kicked Boyd's gun into the corner of the saloon, then joined Ryan in grabbing Boyd.

Each man grabbed an arm and swung Boyd round. They marched him to the door and, on the count of three, kicked him through the batwings.

'Seems it's head first again,' Dalton said, peering over the door.

As the onlookers crowded around the bar, Boyd rolled to a halt in the road. But as he regained his feet, he saw Sheriff Quentin striding purposefully down the road towards him.

Boyd edged from foot to foot then, with a glare at Dalton and an angry slap of a fist against his thigh, turned and hurried towards his horse.

Dalton and Ryan chuckled as Boyd mounted his steed, swung it round, and galloped out of town, Quentin's shouted demands leaving him in no doubt that he wasn't welcome in Yellow Creek again.

'Reckon we won't see him again,' Dalton said as he headed outside.

'And I reckon you're right,' a voice drawled from Dalton's side.

Dalton turned to see that Hunter was leaning on the saloon wall by the door, grinning beneath his lowered hat. Lined up beside him were Gus and the other three men.

'Why are you so interested in my business?' Dalton asked.

Hunter pushed himself from the wall to stand before Dalton.

'Because you rode into town with a bulging carpet-bag, went into the bank, and when you came out, that carpet-bag didn't bulge no more.' Hunter tipped back his hat and set his hands on his hips, but the grin remained. 'You're a right interesting man.'

'Trouble is, you ain't.' Dalton turned and with Ryan at his side, walked into the road.

Hunter uttered more taunts, but Dalton firmed his shoulders and returned to the hotel.

Inside, Ryan bid his goodnights. In the corner of the reception room, he raised a trapdoor, then paced down the steps and into the cellar in which he slept.

Dalton turned to the stairs. Wallace wasn't at the reception desk as he wandered past.

'That's far enough,' a voice muttered from behind the desk.

Dalton swirled round to see Deputy Vaughn rise up from behind the desk, his gun aimed at Dalton's chest.

'I wondered when you'd find me,' Dalton said, backing away a pace. 'But you were slower than I expected.'

At Vaughn's instruction, Dalton raised his hands to chest level.

'I followed your tracks,' Vaughn said, pacing out from behind the reception desk. 'But you switched horses.'

'It was something like that.'

'It don't matter why. You're coming with me.' Vaughn gestured with his gun towards the hotel door.

With no choice, Dalton turned and strode towards the door.

Vaughn filed in behind him, walking five paces back. But then he grunted. Dalton swirled round to see that Ryan had emerged from the cellar and had jumped him, then grabbed Vaughn's gun hand and pushed it high.

The weapon squirmed from Vaughn's grip as Dalton dashed to Ryan's side and, on the run, slammed a blow to Vaughn's chin that crashed him back, tumbling both him and Ryan to the floor.

Even as Vaughn was skidding to a halt, Dalton ripped his gun from its holster and aimed it down at Vaughn.

And when Vaughn extricated himself from Ryan's grip, it was to peer down the barrel of Dalton's gun.

'Go on, shoot,' he muttered.

'I ain't a killer.' Dalton gestured for Ryan to move away from Vaughn, then paced around him until he faced the door. 'And I won't hurt you.'

Vaughn knelt and turned to keep facing Dalton, then spread his hands.

'Then what *will* you do with me?'

Dalton glanced at Ryan, who shrugged. 'I got no—'

Vaughn leapt to his feet and, with his head down, charged Dalton.

Caught in a moment of indecision, Dalton didn't fire and Vaughn bundled into him, knocking him to the floor.

They skidded back along the polished floor towards the open cellar door, but, as Vaughn lunged for Dalton's gun, Dalton thrust up a flat palm to the underside of Vaughn's chin, cracking his head back. Then he kicked up, wheeling Vaughn over his head.

Vaughn hit the floor on his rump and skidded towards the cellar door. He teetered, waving his arms as he fought for balance, but then slipped and crashed down the cellar steps to the bottom.

On his knees, Dalton crawled to the cellar door and peered down. Ryan had taken a light downstairs and, by the sallow light, Dalton could see that Vaughn lay supine at the bottom of the steps.

Even so, he stalked down the steps, his gun drawn. When he reached the bottom step, he saw

Vaughn's slack mouth and the wide white arcs in his eyes.

Still, he confirmed that he was out cold and nothing worse.

As he stood, Ryan joined him, a coil of rope in hand.

'What are we going to do with him?' he asked.

'Got no idea.' Dalton considered Ryan. 'But aren't you going to ask why he was after me?'

Ryan shook his head. Dalton patted Ryan's back then, as there'd be witnesses if he took Vaughn outside, investigated the cellar. He confirmed the trap-door was the only way into the room and that, judging by the dead rats and the stench of decay, Wallace never stored anything down here.

So, Dalton grabbed Vaughn's arms and dragged him behind a stack of mouldering crates in the corner.

'You should leave now,' Ryan said. 'I'll keep him company until you're long gone.'

'Obliged for the offer, but he's relentless. I need Raphael's fifty dollars so that I can buy provisions and hide out for a long, long time.' Dalton stood back to consider the crates. He reckoned that somebody could walk within four feet of Vaughn and not notice him. 'But as soon as the deal is over, I'll leave.'

CHAPTER 8

On the day of the hotel deal, Dalton woke at sun-up and, as Ryan was already attending to his duties, checked on Vaughn.

He hunkered down before the bound and gagged man.

Vaughn peered at him over his gag and struggled within his bonds, but on finding them secure, relented and lay back, glaring up at Dalton.

Dalton mimed a knife running across his throat, then reached out to remove Vaughn's gag, but stopped with the fingers inches from the cloth.

Vaughn looked up at him, then nodded. With an outstretched finger, Dalton prised the gag down from Vaughn's mouth.

'You enjoying your stay at the Hotel Splendour?' he asked.

'I ain't,' Vaughn grunted. 'But it gives me another reason to make you suffer.'

'There's no need. I got no desire to kill you. I'm leaving. But I've arranged for someone to free you later.'

'You'll never get far enough away from me, Dalton. Not now, not ever.'

'Ever is a long time. But I guess I could leave you down here to rot for ever.'

'I thought you said you'd let me go, but I guess there's no reasoning with the likes of you.'

Dalton lowered his head. 'And I guess there's no reasoning with you, either.'

Dalton drew the gag back over Vaughn's mouth, then turned and, without a backward glance, left the cellar.

Upstairs, he looked in on Raphael, and over breakfast, Raphael gave him his instructions as to how he would ensure today's deal went smoothly.

And, as always, those instructions were precise.

So, for the rest of the morning, Dalton stayed in his room with the door to the adjoining room open, ensuring that nobody came in, even to clean.

At eleven o'clock precisely he went downstairs to see Wallace, who was pacing up and down the reception room, wringing his hands and glancing at his watch on every circuit of the room. From him, he obtained the spare keys to his and to Raphael's rooms. He also obtained the keys to the rooms on either side of those rooms, and even checked that these rooms were, in fact, unoccupied.

Then he went to the bank and withdrew the sum total of Raphael's deposited funds. He watched the teller count out the exact amount, then deposited it in the same carpet-bag in which he'd delivered the

$800 yesterday. He instructed the teller that the cash would return within the hour, but under a different ownership.

Then he headed outside. On the boardwalk, he glanced along the road. Hunter's less than subtle comments hinted that he might try to snatch the money, but as he didn't see anyone looking at him, Dalton slung the carpet-bag over his shoulder and strode across the road and into the hotel.

On the second floor, Dalton knocked three times on Raphael's door, receiving an answering rap, then entered the room and locked the door behind him. He acknowledged Raphael, then went into the adjoining room; again he locked the door behind him. He checked that the door to the corridor was locked, then placed the carpet-bag in the room's wardrobe, which was in the far corner. He locked the wardrobe, then stood before it.

Nobody could see that he stood before the wardrobe, guarding it, but Raphael's instructions were most explicit that he should stand there. And, in Dalton's one day of employment, he'd learnt that doing exactly what Raphael said was the best policy.

And as he stood, he saw that from that position he could see both doors and the window. And although the room lacked a veranda, it was the best place to ensure that nobody visited the room unexpectedly.

For forty minutes, Dalton stood. Then Raphael knocked on the adjoining room door – two sharp raps followed by a loud knock.

When Dalton returned a knock, he received a

single knock in return. Then he removed the bag from the wardrobe and, with it slung over his right shoulder, entered Raphael's room.

Two paces in from the door, Raphael stood with his eyebrows raised.

'Everything fine?' he asked.

'No problems,' Dalton said, locking the door behind him.

Raphael nodded, then paced to the writing-desk before the window and, with Dalton's help, dragged it into the centre of the room. He fussed around it, moving the desk a few inches to the side so that it aligned with the window. Then moved the two chairs at the desk so that one faced the door and one faced the window.

He stood back from this minor alteration and declared himself happy, then sat at the desk, facing the door.

After five minutes of silent sitting, the door rattled, followed by some harrumphing from outside, but to Raphael's gesture, Dalton unlocked the door to find Wallace standing in the corridor.

Wallace wiped the sweat from his damp brow, then shuffled into the room.

'You are one minute late,' Raphael said, glaring at the watch in his right hand.

'Am I?' With a shaking hand, Wallace extracted his watch from his waistcoat pocket and glanced at it. 'I reckon I'm one minute early.'

'You are not. But no matter. Have you agreed to my terms?'

'I have.'

'And have you written them out *exactly*, as I specified?'

'I have.'

'Show me.' Raphael thrust out a hand, palm up.

Wallace shuffled to the desk and sat, leaving Dalton to lock the door behind him. From his pocket, Wallace extracted a folded contract and placed it on Raphael's palm, but he didn't release it.

'And I also reckon that it's time for you to pay up.'

Raphael peered at Wallace, the long moment extracting a bead of perspiration from Wallace's brow. Wallace swiped it away and sat tall, but Raphael let a smile appear, then clicked his fingers.

Dalton paced to the desk and when he dropped the carpet-bag beside Wallace with a satisfying thud, Wallace released his grip of the contract.

'I hope you don't mind cash,' Raphael said, flicking open the contract with a sharp snap. 'It removes all that waiting for the banks to finalize their administrative details.'

Wallace licked his lips. 'Cash is acceptable.'

'Then count it while I check the contract.'

Dalton snapped open the bag and, with a grin threatening to consume his face, Wallace removed a wad of bills and counted them, his fingers whirling with the practised skill of teller.

For his part, Raphael stared at the contract, reading every word with his eyes narrowed to slits as if one of the legal terms might leap out and attack him.

Wallace riffled through the last wad, then threw it

back into the bag.

'This is all in order,' he said, smiling. 'And you?'

Raphael looked up, his jaw set firm, then stabbed a firm finger on the contract.

'This is *not* in order.'

Wallace's smile died. Then he blinked his shock away and leapt from his chair to stand at Raphael's side.

'What's wrong? Show me, show me.' He ripped his kerchief from his pocket and mopped his cheeks, then his brow. 'This is all what we agreed. It is. It is. I know it is.'

'And it is plainly *not* what we agreed.' Raphael slammed the contract to the desk, then leapt to his feet and stalked to the window, patting a clenched fist against his leg with every pace. 'I believed you to be an honourable man. We agreed to deal gentleman to gentleman with no lawyers looking over our shoulders, just two equals agreeing a contract in exchange for money and a business. But clearly I was wrong.'

Wallace glanced at Dalton, who shrugged, then at the contract. He read it through, hurling the pages back and forth, then gulped and turned to Raphael, his face crumpled and beseeching.

'I *am* dealing with you gentleman to gentleman. This is all what we agreed. If I made a mistake, I . . .' Wallace snuffled a strangulated sob into his kerchief. 'Oh, calamity, I knew something would go wrong.'

'Then you should have been more precise.'

'I guess I'm not so careful with details as you are.

70

Just tell me what's wrong and I'll put it right. Tell me, tell me, please.'

Raphael turned from the window and lifted on his heels.

'It is the last term. You are handing over your land and your railroad stock.'

'I am. I am.'

'But I specifically told you to exclude the livestock you have somehow acquired.'

Wallace blinked. 'You specifically told me to *include* them.'

'I did not.'

'You told me . . .' Wallace gulped as Raphael flared his eyes. 'I'm sure that you said that. . . . At least I think that you said that . . . .'

Raphael sighed and raised a hand. 'There is no point arguing about it. If you are telling me that you made an honest mistake, I will believe you. What is done, is done.'

'It *was* an honest mistake.'

'Then we need to decide what to do next.'

Wallace grinned and jumped on the spot, then frowned.

'And what do we do next?'

Raphael looked at Dalton. 'Dave, leave us while we decide how to address this *mistake*.'

Dalton nodded and grabbed the bag. Wallace watched him close the bag, a hint of moisture in his eyes, but Dalton hefted it on his shoulder and strode into the adjoining room, locking it behind him.

Raphael had given him instructions as to what he

71

should do if the contract signing failed. So, he locked the bag in the wardrobe, checked that the door to the corridor was still locked, then stood before the wardrobe.

For thirty minutes, he listened to the subdued conversation in the next room, but cramps eventually forced him to sit back in the chair beside the window.

Then, next door, Wallace – Dalton presumed it was he from the heavy footfalls – left the room and returned. The tinkling of crockery implied that he also returned with food and drink, but nobody knocked on the door to offer Dalton anything.

After an hour, a short series of laughs sounded, followed by the bustle of someone clearing away the crockery. Then two sharp knocks sounded on the door. Dalton jumped to his feet, unlocked the wardrobe and, with the carpet-bag in hand, left the room.

Raphael was standing in the middle of his room, smiling. Ryan was tidying away the plates while Wallace was rubbing his hands together and grinning.

'We are back on schedule,' Raphael said, waving a ten-dollar bill.

Dalton raised his eyebrows. 'You queried a two-thousand-dollar contract for ten dollars?'

'Precision is the secret of my success. I act in a precise order, and I always succeed.' Raphael waggled a finger at Dalton. 'You will be wise to note that if you wish to be a success, too.'

Dalton nodded and swung the bag on to the writing-desk.

While licking his lips, Wallace eyed the bag, but as he reached for it, Raphael held out his hand for the contract.

Wallace slapped the contract into Raphael's hand. With a flourish, Raphael signed at the bottom, but as he stood aside, Wallace opened the bag and reached for the topmost wad of bills.

Raphael tutted and tapped a foot on the floor, his impatience forcing Wallace to close the bag and add his own signature. Then Wallace blew on the ink and stared at it as if he was willing it to dry faster. He shook the contract, then handed it to Raphael, who returned a short bow.

'The sum of two thousand one hundred and *five* dollars,' Raphael said, waving the ten-dollar bill, 'is yours.'

'And the Hotel Splendour is yours,' Wallace said, his voice breaking. Then he punched the air. 'And I do declare it's time for a celebratory drink.'

'Only when you have banked the money. Dave, show Wallace the same care you have shown me.'

'No trouble,' Dalton said. He grabbed the bag and turned towards the door, then glanced at Wallace. 'If that's all right with you.'

'Well . . .' Wallace tipped back his hat to scratch his head. 'On second thoughts, Ryan will accompany me. No offence, Dave, but I've known him longer than you.'

Dalton shrugged, then held out the bag to Ryan,

who took it and headed to the door with Wallace pacing behind him.

'You can trust Dave,' Raphael said, but his offer didn't halt Wallace. 'I trusted him with my money and his behaviour is impeccable.'

'I've got all the help I need,' Wallace said as he followed Ryan into the corridor.

'Still, he would be helpful.'

In the corridor, Wallace grunted an order to Ryan, then swung back around the door.

'The money is no longer yours. I'll deal with it.'

'Wallace,' Raphael muttered, 'I *really* think Dave should ensure nothing untoward happens to your money.'

'I should,' Dalton murmured. 'Some rough types were showing an interest and—'

Wallace raised a hand. 'Say no more. I'd welcome your help in looking out for these rough types.'

Dalton nodded and followed Wallace, but in the corridor, Wallace glanced left and right, bleated a pained screech, then dashed to the stairs.

'What's wrong?' Dalton asked, hurrying after him.

'Ryan isn't here,' Wallace whined, skidding to a halt at the top of the stairs.

'He must have . . .' Dalton winced as he joined Wallace. The stairs were clear.

'You looking for me?' Ryan said, pacing out from room eighteen.

'What were you doing in there?' Wallace shouted, swirling round on the spot.

Ryan held the bag high. 'I thought it best not to

stand around in the corridor with all this money.'

'Yeah, I suppose.' Wallace slapped a hand to his chest. 'Just don't give me any more shocks. I've had enough for one day.'

Ryan glanced at Dalton and furrowed his brow, but Dalton returned an exasperated shake of his head.

Then they headed down the stairs with Wallace leading, Ryan in the middle, and Dalton walking a few paces back.

On their way, Wallace maintained a continuous stream of nervous chatter over his shoulder to Ryan. But Dalton didn't listen, concentrating instead on looking out for Hunter, or anyone else who might try to part Wallace from the proceeds of the hotel sale.

But they paced through the hotel, outside, and across the road without anyone showing any interest in them.

With Wallace in the lead, they entered the bank, but as Dalton followed him inside, he noticed the subdued atmosphere. The customers and teller were standing still and engaging in low, animated conversation.

Then Hunter emerged from beside the door, his gun drawn and aimed at Dalton's chest.

Dalton side-stepped and scrambled for his gun, but a firm hand gripped his forearm from behind and levered his arm up. Dalton struggled to free himself, but his unseen assailant wrapped another arm around his neck and pulled him back against the barrel of a gun.

Ryan dropped the bag at his feet and swung round to confront Hunter, his hand swinging to his holster, but to a grunted order from Dalton, he didn't grab his gun and instead, raised his hands.

With a bleat of alarm, Wallace crumpled to his knees.

'Oh, calamity,' he whined. 'Do something, Dave.'

The man holding Dalton thrust the cold metal into the small of his back, forcing Dalton to shake his head.

'Dave ain't stupid,' Hunter said, pacing across the bank. 'He doesn't want to die, and if you got the same desire, Ryan, you'll kick that bag to me.'

Ryan glanced at Dalton, and when Dalton returned a reluctant nod, he kicked the bag to Hunter's feet. Hunter gestured for Gus to pick it up.

As Wallace whimpered, Gus grabbed the bag, then ripped it open.

'What's this?' he grunted, looking down at Wallace.

'The money from the sale of my hotel.' On his knees, Wallace gulped, strangulating a sob, then waggled a finger at Gus. 'But I'll get it back, just see if I don't.'

'The money, *now*,' Gus muttered.

'That is the . . .'

Gus grunted his annoyance. He held the bag out to Wallace, who scrambled along the floor and peered inside, then staggered to his feet, a hand clutching his chest.

'What's wrong?' Hunter asked, pushing Wallace aside.

Gus upended the bag and emptied its contents on to the floor. A mound of bundled and sliced newspaper grew at his feet.

'The money ain't in here,' he grunted. 'The money just ain't here.'

'Yeah,' Wallace whined. 'It just ain't here.'

CHAPTER 9

'The bag was full of *what?*' Raphael said, slamming his hands on his hips.

'Newspaper,' Wallace whined. 'It was full of cut newspaper. There wasn't a single dollar bill in there.'

'No money at all?'

'None.'

Raphael paced to the window of his hotel room and stood before the window, lifting on his heels and shaking his head.

'Then, cheer up. At least that outlaw didn't steal anything.'

'Quit baiting me, Raphael. I see nothing funny about this.'

'Then if it isn't funny, it is most unfortunate.'

'Unfortunate isn't the word I'd use to describe it.' Wallace bit his knuckle, but a strangulated oath still escaped.

The last ten minutes had been fraught.

Hunter and his hapless outlaws had tried to slap the truth out of Wallace, but Wallace's plaintive wail-

ing left them in no doubt that the absence of cash
had surprised him as much as it had annoyed them.
So, with much glowering and posturing, they had left
the bank and galloped out of Yellow Creek.

Although no actual crime had occurred, the teller
had called for Sheriff Quentin. While they waited for
him, the teller had laughed, regaling everyone with
additional details of the worst bank raid he'd ever
witnessed.

But Wallace had seen nothing funny in the inci-
dent and had conducted a furious argument with
Ryan, Dalton, the teller, and anyone else who'd made
the mistake of straying too close to him.

Then he'd hurled the empty carpet-bag to the
floor and dashed back to the hotel with Dalton trailing behind him. Ryan had stayed behind to explain
what had happened to Sheriff Quentin.

Since returning to the hotel, Wallace had just
stayed on the side of decorum, but from his rapidly
reddening face, Dalton reckoned that was about to
change.

'And what word would you use?' Raphael asked.

'Robbery, deception, fraud.' Wallace waved his
arms above his head, then pointed a firm finger at
Raphael. 'And I can think of plenty more to describe
what you've just tried.'

Raphael arched an eyebrow. 'I've tried nothing.'

'You tried to steal my hotel using the most . . . most
pathetic trick I've ever heard of.'

'Wallace,' Dalton said, pacing to his side, 'you got
to think straight. You've accused pretty much every-

body in Yellow Creek of stealing your money. You have to think this through before you jump to another hasty conclusion.'

'I have thought this through,' Wallace shouted. 'That man tried to buy my hotel with a bag full of newspaper.'

'Listen to Dave,' Raphael said. 'These accusations are doing you no good while you are not thinking clearly.'

'I am thinking clearly. You tried to . . .' Wallace's eyes glazed. Then he paced round on the spot with his head lowered and a finger patting his chin. He looked up, nodding. 'But that isn't it, is it? This is another one of your delaying tactics to drive the price down. But it won't work. I've had enough of being used, and you will pay me in real money or leave my hotel this minute.'

'The bag contained real money. You opened the bag and saw it.'

As Ryan wandered into the room, Wallace glanced at Dalton. His eyes narrowed.

'You were in the other room with the bag,' he said, speaking slowly, 'but the room was locked. The only other time the money left my sight was when . . .' Wallace swirled round to face Ryan. '. . . was when you left this room. And you disappeared for a full minute.'

Ryan staggered back a pace, his eyes boggling. He glanced at each man in the room, receiving a head-shake and a mouthed plea for calm from Dalton, but a firm glare from the other two. He backed away towards the door.

'I didn't steal it,' he murmured.

'Now,' Raphael said, 'we're getting to the truth.'

'So, why did you hide in room eighteen?' Wallace said, pacing round to stand between Ryan and the door. 'After I told you to stay in the corridor.'

'I explained. I was just . . .' Ryan closed his eyes a moment. 'You can't accuse me. I'm no thief.'

As Wallace glared at Ryan, seemingly trying to extract a confession using only his accusing gaze, the door swung open and Sheriff Quentin strode in.

Ryan glanced at the sheriff, then at Wallace. He gulped, then barged Wallace aside, and dashed through the door, slamming it shut behind him.

'Don't run!' Dalton shouted, taking a long pace towards the door, but Quentin stood before him.

'Nobody else leaves,' he said, 'until someone tells me what's happened.'

'A robbery, that's what's happened,' Wallace whined. 'Ryan stole two thousand dollars.'

'Two thousand dollars!' Quentin pointed at each man in the room in turn. 'Stay here. I'll deal with this.'

Quentin drew his gun and danced back through the door. Dalton moved to follow him, but Raphael shook his head.

'Dave, let the lawman catch Ryan, and then we'll all know what happened to Wallace's money.'

'If Ryan stole anyone's money,' Wallace said, 'it was yours.'

'That was *your* money.' Raphael raised a hand as Wallace muttered an oath. 'But that isn't important now. We should wait until Sheriff Quentin has locked Ryan away. Then we can discuss what we do next.'

Wallace sighed and threw himself into a chair beside the door.

'This day just keeps getting worse and worse,' he whined.

'Is he talking?' Raphael asked.

Sheriff Quentin paced into Raphael's room, leaving Deputy Swanson in the corridor, and shook his head.

'Ryan is in the same surly mood that all men are in when you arrest them. But he's hiding something, that's for sure.'

'Just because Ryan ran,' Dalton said, 'it doesn't mean he's guilty.'

'And just because a man doesn't run, it doesn't mean he's innocent.' Quentin stared at Dalton, but Dalton returned his gaze. 'But while I wait for him to talk, it'd sure help if I could find the money. He didn't have long to stash two thousand dollars. Where did he go while he was out of your sight?'

Wallace drew Quentin to the door and pointed down the corridor.

'Room eighteen.'

'Then we'll start there.' Quentin ordered Deputy Swanson to search room eighteen.

'He could have had an accomplice,' Raphael said. 'And passed the money on to him.'

'He could have,' Wallace murmured. He glanced at Quentin. 'But before you go, I'd be obliged if you'd settle the biggest argument we have here. Whose money did Ryan steal?'

Quentin tipped back his hat. 'I don't know all the details of your business contract, but either way, you'll need a lawyer to settle that one.'

Wallace removed his hat to mop his brow.

'Then just give me your opinion.'

Quentin stared into the corridor, not meeting anyone's gaze.

'From what I've heard, you received a bag of money, but somebody, probably Ryan, stole it before you banked it.'

Raphael grunted his agreement, but Wallace raised a finger.

'*If* the money was still in the bag when I signed the contract.'

'You cannot continue claiming that,' Raphael muttered. 'We all saw that the money was in the bag.'

'I thought I saw a wad of bills on the top of the bag.' Wallace slammed a fist into his palm. 'But that could have been a trick of the light, or there could have been real money on the outside of the wads, and the rest could have been cut newspaper.'

For long moments, everyone stood in silence. Then Quentin coughed.

'You signed a contract to sell all your business interests,' he intoned, 'and you didn't check that you were receiving any cash in return?'

Wallace gulped, then lowered his head.

'I guess when you put it like that, I wasn't too clever.'

'It's the stupidest thing I've ever heard. I'd keep quiet about your suspicions if I were you.' Quentin wandered out, shaking his head, and down the corridor.

'And you *will* keep quiet,' Raphael said, his voice low. 'I will not have such rumours spreading. I am an honest businessman, who has seen another honest businessman robbed. I sympathize, but I will not let you besmirch my name.'

'I'm sorry,' Wallace whispered, his voice barely audible, then wandered to the door. 'This has been a rough day.'

As Wallace slouched into the corridor, Raphael glanced at Dalton.

Ensure he stops complaining.'

Dalton nodded and paced to the door, but stopped in the doorway.

'I got to ask you something,' he said, turning. 'You're not worried about that rumour being true, are you?'

'No, but I am worried about Ryan. He's a nice man.'

Raphael considered Dalton, then shrugged.

'Ryan is a thief.'

Dalton shook his head, then headed into the corridor.

CHAPTER 10

While Deputy Swanson searched the hotel, starting in room eighteen, Dalton searched for a barrel.

When he found one in the alley behind the hotel, he rolled it through the kitchen and into the cellar, then dragged Vaughn out from behind the stack of crates.

Vaughn glared at him, his eyes wide and accusing, but Dalton grabbed his chin and held it high, then slugged his jaw, slamming his head back on to the floor.

If Swanson's search was thorough, he would locate any hiding-place in the hotel, but taking Vaughn from the cellar with so many people around was impossible.

So, he had to trust that Swanson wasn't too thorough and that Vaughn didn't stir too quickly.

He checked Vaughn was out cold, then dumped him in the barrel and placed the most mouldering rags he could find on top of him. Then, to reduce the chances of investigation, he laid two rank-smelling dead rats on top of the rags, arranging them beside the slightly open lid, implying they'd crawled inside to die some time ago.

With the barrel tucked in the corner, Dalton climbed out of the cellar and, as nobody was in the reception room, left the hotel.

On the boardwalk, he turned towards the sheriff's office.

But loud footfalls pattered behind him.

He swirled round, but a sack landed over his head and rough hands pulled him backwards. Dalton lunged out, but at least two people held him in a secure arm-lock. With no choice, he postponed resisting, but even with his sight gone, Dalton reckoned his assailants were dragging him down the alley beside the hotel and beyond.

Only when they'd stopped and Dalton smelled a nearby horse did he accept their intent. He went limp, but when they moved to drag him on to the horse, he hurled his arms out and, in a berserk action, threw the men away from him, then ripped the sack from his head.

Dalton found that he was facing Hunter, his four men flanking him.

'I ain't going nowhere with you,' he said, edging towards the alley.

'Two thousand dollars is missing,' Hunter said, pacing to the side to block his route, 'and you know where it is.'

Dalton snorted and stepped away from Hunter, but Gus grabbed his arm and pulled him back.

Dalton ripped his arm away, but the men moved in to surround him.

'I don't.'

'Then we'll see how long it takes us to change that story.'

Hunter gestured and two men lunged for him, but Dalton danced back, their grasps closing on air.

The other men were blocking his route to the back of the alley so Dalton charged Hunter, hitting him full in the chest with his leading shoulder and slamming him on to his back. Dalton avoided falling and stood straight, but hands grabbed him from behind. He thrust his arms out, but this time, the hands had grabbed a firmer grip, so Dalton slammed his feet to the ground and bent himself double.

With his back braced, he lifted the man behind him off the ground and hurled him over his shoulder. Both men tumbled to the ground, but Dalton kept the roll going and came up facing the horse. He dashed two long paces towards it, forcing the remaining standing men to hurry in stop him, but then skidded to a halt and dashed in the opposite direction towards the alley.

Only one man stood in his way.

Dalton feinted to go left, but when the man danced to the side to block him, he side-stepped and went right instead. But the man kicked up, his boot connecting with Dalton's leg.

Dalton went down, but turned the fall into a roll over his shoulder and came up on his feet.

The man lunged for his arm, but Dalton swung

round and slapped his face with a mixture of elbow and forearm, freeing himself, then hurtled into the alley.

Firm footfalls charged after him, but Dalton thrust his head down and pounded down the alley.

'Halt, or you get a bullet in the back,' Hunter shouted from behind him, but Dalton thrust his head down and sprinted with all his might down the alley.

With every pace, he expected Hunter to fire, but he pounded the last ten paces, then threw himself to the ground, rolling over a shoulder as he tumbled around the corner. He lay on the edge of the board-walk, receiving several bemused looks from passers-by, then ventured a glance back into the alley, but Hunter and his men were no longer there.

Dalton stood with his back to the wall, but distant and irritated shouting suggested that Hunter was now rounding up his men to leave town.

So Dalton batted the dust from his knees and, with a roll of the shoulders, resumed the journey that he'd intended to make before Hunter had ambushed him. He crossed the road to the sheriff's office.

With Swanson searching the hotel, Quentin was the only lawman on duty.

'You got more information?' Quentin said, look-ing up from his desk.

Dalton glanced at the cells. In the corner cell, Ryan sat on his bunk with his legs drawn up to his chin, but he didn't look up to acknowledge that he'd heard Dalton enter.

'Nope,' Dalton said. 'But I do want to speak to Ryan.'

Quentin drew Dalton to his desk, out of Ryan's eyeline.

'Why?' he asked. 'He still ain't being talkative.'

'To you, maybe not. But he might talk to me.'

For long moments, Quentin stared at Dalton, then nodded and held out his hand for Dalton's gun.

Quentin paced to the corner, unlocked the cell door, and stood aside for Dalton to enter Ryan's cell. He locked the door and stood beside it, but when Dalton and Ryan just stared at each other in silence, he snorted and backed out of earshot.

Ryan swung his feet down from his bunk, but set them apart and hunched his body so that his gaze was on the floor.

'This is a right fine mess, Ryan,' Dalton said.

For long moments, Ryan didn't reply, and when he did, his voice was a croaked whisper.

'That's true.'

'You comfortable?'

'Yeah.'

'Do you need anything? Quentin might not let me bring it in, but I can ask.'

'I don't need nothing.' Ryan looked up to face Dalton for the first time. 'Dave, why are you here?'

Dalton stood beside Ryan and leaned on the cell bars.

'To help you.'

Ryan slapped his knee, then jumped to his feet.

He stalked to the cell door, slapped a bar, turned, and paced to the side wall. He gripped the bars, staring through the cell next to him at Quentin, then swirled round and threw himself back on to his bunk.

'Don't waste your time on me,' he whispered. 'You got problems of your own. Just leave town.'

'And I will when I've helped to free you.'

'Obliged for the thought, but I'm in deep trouble.'

'And that's all the more reason for me to help you. You didn't steal the money.'

Ryan stared up at the ceiling. 'You can't know that.'

'I know you. And I know some of the other people in that hotel. There's a better explanation here than that you stole the money.'

'I deserve to be punished. I did wrong.'

'You saying you did steal the money?' Dalton stared down at Ryan, but Ryan snorted and rolled on his bunk to turn his back on him. 'Just tell me if you did. I won't tell Quentin until I've figured out a way to help you. But you have to tell me the truth.'

'The truth is bad. And I can't tell you what it is.' Ryan rolled back to stare up at Dalton. 'And a wanted man will know why that is.'

Dalton glanced away to confirm that Quentin was out of hearing range.

'I know what happens when someone hears part of a story and assumes other things about you.' Dalton rubbed his chin. 'Are you saying that you're a wanted man, and that you'd sooner take the punishment for stealing two thousand dollars than tell your full story and risk more?'

'I'm not saying that. Just go.'

Dalton sat on the edge of Ryan's bunk.

'Tell me. The truth can't shock me.'

Ryan took a deep breath and, in his impassive face, Dalton reckoned he could read the type of thoughts that were knocking back and forth. Ryan was scared. He'd done something terrible. He didn't know whom he could trust.

But just as Ryan nodded with a hint of trust in his eyes, Deputy Swanson burst into the sheriff's office and demanded that Quentin go to the hotel immediately.

Quentin ordered Swanson to release Dalton from the cell, then dashed outside.

Ryan craned his neck. 'What you reckon he's found?'

'Something to prove your innocence, I reckon.' Dalton gulped. 'Or Vaughn.'

Ryan slammed a hand on Dalton's arm. 'Then forget me, Dave. You only have a few minutes. Put as much distance between Yellow Creek and him as you can.'

Ryan gripped his hand more tightly, then sat back on his bunk.

Dalton shared eye-contact with Ryan until Swanson opened the door. He headed to the door, but stopped in the doorway and turned.

'Ryan, no matter what happens, someone has framed you for this robbery, and I intend to discover who that person is.'

Swanson slapped a hand on Dalton's shoulder and tugged him from the door, but Dalton dug his heels in and continued to stare at Ryan until he looked up at him.

'Don't, Dave. Just go. Nobody would frame the likes of me. I'm just a bellboy.'

Dalton winced, and when Swanson gripped his shoulder more tightly, he let him lead him from the cell.

'And you're right,' he said as Swanson locked the cell. 'Nobody would frame the likes of *you*.'

When Dalton left the sheriff's office, he stood on the boardwalk and stared at the hotel. From outside, the hotel was as serene as always, giving no hints as to whether Swanson had discovered Vaughn.

Dalton glanced down the road to the livery stable, then shook his head and strode across the road to the hotel.

Inside, the staff were hurtling back and forth, a hubbub of chatter rippling.

But everyone was milling around the cellar door.

Dalton winced and backed to the main door, torn between his desire to escape and his need to stay and help Ryan.

But Wallace emerged from the group and waved to him.

'Great news,' he shouted, making Dalton stop and turn. 'Quentin has proved Ryan is guilty.'

Dalton glanced at the cellar door to see Quentin emerge and wave a bundle of bills above his head.

'Swanson found this,' he said, pacing to Wallace's side, 'under Ryan's bedding – one hundred dollars. And it won't be long before I find the rest.'

Dalton glanced at the open cellar door.

'You find anything else down there?'

'Nope, I searched the cellar from top to bottom, but the rest of the money is close, I can feel it.'

With the success of finding some of what appeared to be the stolen money, Wallace was keen for Quentin to search the hotel in greater depth. But before the sheriff could start, Raphael emerged from his room and objected to the disruption in his hotel.

As the terms of the hotel sale contract, and so the ownership of the hotel, were still in question, Wallace and Raphael went into the office to argue, leaving Quentin and Dalton in the reception room.

'Did Ryan talk?' Quentin asked.

'Not yet,' Dalton said. 'But I'm sure he didn't steal the money.'

'And you're saying that after Swanson found that one hundred dollars?'

'*Especially* after Swanson found that one hundred dollars. I just don't reckon Ryan had enough time to stash the money in the cellar.'

'And why would a bellboy who dreams of nickel-and-dime tips have one hundred dollars hidden under his bed?'

'I don't know, but when I do, I'll also know who really stole the two thousand dollars.'

Quentin snorted, then swung round to stand before Dalton.

'Stay out of this, Dave. After your success in free-ing Stirling Kimball, I don't need you meddling in another one of my investigations.'

Quentin slammed his hands on his hips and stared at Dalton, but when Dalton just returned his own level gaze, he turned and left the hotel.

When the door shut behind Quentin, Dalton dashed down the cellar steps. The barrel was still in the corner. Dalton stalked towards it, half-expecting Vaughn to leap out. But when he threw back the lid, the mouldering rags and rats lay on the bottom.

And Vaughn had gone.

Dalton threw the rags to the floor, revealing lengths of cut rope with frayed ends. A glint caught his eye, so he reached in and fingered the slither of glass that must have been trapped in the rags.

As Vaughn hadn't immediately gone to Sheriff Quentin, Dalton assumed that he would never do this. But with no choice but to put this problem from his mind and try to prove Ryan's innocence as quickly as possible, he climbed the steps to the recep-tion room.

As Wallace and Raphael were still arguing, he considered the room keys behind the reception desk, but as Raphael still had the keys for both his own and Dalton's room, he couldn't go up to his room.

But a key for the adjoining room eighteen was there.

Dalton now remembered that he'd also given the keys to the rooms surrounding room sixteen and seventeen to Raphael. But Ryan had hidden in the supposedly locked room eighteen. With no clear idea as to how this could have happened, Dalton took the key and went upstairs.

Dalton glanced up and down the corridor, ensuring nobody saw him, then entered the room.

He looked around, confirming that the room was identical to his room, except the large wardrobe was in the opposite corner.

Although he was still unsure as to what he was looking for, he paced around the room, then peered through the window at the road below. Then he turned and stood with his back to the window to face into the room.

Again, the large wardrobe drew his attention. It was the only item of furniture that was in a different place from the one in the room next door, and for that matter, the one in Raphael's room, too.

He opened the wardrobe and peered inside. It was bare, but the back board was propped against the wall and scuff marks around the side suggested that someone had prised it away, then hastily replaced it.

Dalton pulled the board back. Beyond was the wall. Dalton stood back and decided that this length of wall would back up to the wardrobe in the adjoining room, and the place where he'd stored the carpetbag while Raphael's negotiations rumbled on.

With an extended knuckle, Dalton tapped the wall. The noise was hollow, as of hitting thin board. Smiling, he slipped out of the wardrobe and tapped the wall beside the it. He received the kind of solid sound he'd expect from a thick hotel wall.

Dalton slipped back into the wardrobe and felt around the edges of the false wall. His fingers slipped behind it and, with a slight and quiet tug, he pulled it away.

Beyond, was the inside of room seventeen's wardrobe.

Dalton reached in, confirming the ease with which someone could have switched a bag containing two thousand dollars for a bag containing cut newspaper.

Dalton closed the wardrobe, smiling.

'Did you find it?' a voice said from behind him.

Dalton swirled round to see that Raphael Huffman was standing in the doorway.

'I was just searching for trouble, as a good hired gun should.'

Raphael wandered into the room and past Dalton. He opened the wardrobe and peered inside, then closed the doors and stood with his back to them.

'And did my hired gun find any trouble in there?'

'Yeah. I know what really happened now. You distracted Wallace with your arguments about the contract while Boyd sneaked into this room and switched the bag.' Dalton squared up to Raphael, then snorted. 'And now, I'll tell Sheriff Quentin.'

Raphael strode a pace closer to Dalton. 'You won't, if you want to live.'

'Stirling doesn't worry me and I can deal with the likes of Boyd.'

'You only need to worry about me.' Raphael leaned towards Dalton. 'Because I can stop you talking with just one word, Dave.'

Dalton looked Raphael up and down. 'And what word is that?'

Raphael licked his lips and lowered his voice to a whisper.

'Dalton.'

CHAPTER 11

Dalton narrowed his eyes. 'I don't know what you mean.'

'You do,' Raphael said. 'You are pretending to be a man called Dave, but your real name is Dalton – a wanted man.'

Dalton firmed his jaw, trying to avoid swallowing to relieve his rapidly drying throat, but finding that he had to gulp.

'Have you met Deputy Vaughn?'

'Who's he?'

Dalton searched Raphael's eyes, but they didn't flicker with doubt. 'It don't matter. I don't know about this.'

Raphael's eyes flickered with amusement.

'That isn't what Stirling Kimball said.'

Dalton closed his eyes and when he opened them, he met Raphael's gaze.

'He told you about me?'

'Why else do you think he told you to head to the Hotel Splendour for work? We needed the perfect person to take responsibility for stealing the money. And what could be better than a wanted man?'

'So, I *was* the intended culprit,' Dalton mused, 'but Ryan got in the way.'

'He did. But Ryan is plausible. It seems he has secrets, too.'

'Quit gloating and just tell me what you're threatening me with.'

'It's simple. If you tell Sheriff Quentin what you suspect, I will deny everything, and without the evidence of the two thousand dollars, you'll prove nothing.' Raphael smiled. 'And I'll also tell Sheriff Quentin about your past and you'll rot in jail for the rest of your life, as will your friend, Ryan.'

Dalton bit back a sharp oath, his fists clenching and unclenching, then turned on his heel, leaving Raphael in his room.

With his mind in a fugue, he strode along the corridor, down the stairs, and outside.

On the boardwalk, he glanced at the sheriff's office, but then turned and stormed along the boardwalk.

For the next ten minutes, he searched the saloons in Yellow Creek.

In the lowest, dirtiest saloon on the edge of the town, he found Boyd Dooley hunched over the bar and staring into the bottom of his whiskey glass.

He paced to the bar and stood beside him.

From the corner of his eye, Boyd looked at him and snorted. 'On your own?' he said, his voice tired and slurred.

'I don't need help to take you on.'

Boyd feigned a yawn. 'I ain't interested. I got no desire to fight you no more. I've been doing plenty of thinking and I reckon I'm better off not working for Mr . . . that Raphael. You can suffer his demands all day. I don't have to no more.'

'I don't have to do that no more, but *you* are still doing his bidding.' Dalton raised his eyebrows. 'You want to tell me where the two thousand dollars is, or do I have to beat it out of you?'

Boyd fingered his glass, then pushed it from him.

'That ain't wise talk for a man on his own.'

Dalton made a fist and glanced at it.

'The two thousand dollars, now.'

Boyd looked around the saloon. 'If I had two thousand dollars, do you think I'd be drinking in the lowest, dirtiest saloon in town?'

'Quentin ran you out of town. But you came back, and that makes no sense unless you still work for Raphael.'

'And you ain't making sense either.' Boyd pushed a whiskey bottle down the bar to Dalton. 'Drink this. Then go and annoy someone else.'

Boyd pushed himself from the bar and wandered by Dalton. Dalton watched him leave, then followed him outside. In the doorway, he watched Boyd wander down the road and into the stable, then followed him.

He stood in the doorway, letting his shadow block the light until Boyd lowered the saddle he was taking to his horse.

'I ain't leaving you,' Dalton muttered, 'until you help me free Ryan.'

'Then you'll be with me for a long time because I ain't helping you do nothing.'

Dalton rolled his shoulders and paced into the stable to stand before Boyd.

'You'll do what I tell you to do.'

Boyd snorted, then turned to his horse, but then swirled back and swung the saddle round, aiming to slam it into Dalton's chest.

Dalton saw the blow coming and danced back, but it still clipped his shoulder and pushed him back two paces. Dalton dug his heels in, stilling his progress, but Boyd dropped the saddle and charged him, leading with his right shoulder.

Boyd's attack skidded Dalton back four feet, but then Boyd's momentum knocked Dalton's right leg from under him and he crashed down on his back. Before he recovered, Boyd dived on top of him, blasting all the wind from his chest.

Momentarily winded, Dalton floundered on the ground. Through a shaking and blurred vision, he looked up to see Boyd rip back a fist, ready to pummel his face.

Dalton darted his head to the side and the blow crunched into the ground beside his head. The missed blow dragged a pained bleat from Boyd. He leapt to his feet and staggered in a circle, cradling his hand, giving Dalton enough time to jump to his feet and grab Boyd's arm, then dance to the side and fling him at the wall.

Boyd slammed into the wall and rebounded into a right cross that knocked him straight. Only the wall stopped him from falling. Boyd shook himself, then rolled his shoulders and stood tall as he confronted Dalton.

'You just got me mad,' he bellowed. 'Now, you'll suffer.'

Boyd stalked towards Dalton, his hands held out, his body bent double.

'I won't, but you will help me.' Dalton matched Boyd's posture and beckoned him on. 'You're taking me to the money you stole.'

Boyd advanced, but Dalton edged to the side and, ten feet apart, the men circled, each keeping the other man in his gaze.

Boyd was the first to break, darting forward and aiming to grab Dalton in a neck-hold, but Dalton danced back. Boyd's arms flailed through the air and, with Boyd off-balance, Dalton kicked his rump hurtling him to the dirt.

Boyd rolled on to his back, then grunted and jumped to his feet. He charged Dalton.

Again, Dalton danced to the side, but Boyd followed his movement and grabbed him in a bear-hug. Boyd grinned, his eyes bright and, using his superior weight, thrust his arms in, aiming to crush Dalton's ribs.

Dalton squirmed but couldn't free himself, then chopped both hands into the sides of Boyd's bull-like neck. The hands rebounded. He stamped at Boyd's feet, but Boyd had set them well apart.

So Dalton set his own feet close together, then brought his knee up sharply, the knee connecting with eye-watering accuracy. Boyd's eyes rolled back, his hold disappearing in a moment, and he staggered back from Dalton, his legs wobbling.

Dalton righted himself and when Boyd staggered round to face him again, he floored him with a sharp uppercut to the chin that lifted his feet off the ground before he ploughed through the dirt.

Dalton leapt on Boyd and grabbed his collar to lift him high. He pulled back his fist and smashed a soft blow to his cheek which still slammed his head back, then pulled back his fist even harder.

'Now, Boyd,' he grunted, 'do you want me to hit you again, or do you take me to the two thousand?'

'I don't know about no two thousand,' Boyd whined, his watering eyes rolling.

'Wrong answer.' Dalton slammed his fist into Boyd's face then ripped it back again. 'The two thousand, *now.*'

'I don't know about it.'

Dalton pulled back his fist, but Boyd raised a weak hand, halting him.

'And I don't believe you,' Dalton grunted. 'You and Raphael and Stirling are in this together and you *will* give it to me.'

'Stirling *is* working with Raphael, but they don't include me in their plans.' Boyd sighed. 'I just do what Raphael tells me to do.'

'And when he told you to steal two thousand dollars, did you?'

'I did.' Boyd fixed Dalton with a firm gaze. 'But I don't have it now. Stirling has it.'

Dalton raised his fist. 'Then you'll take me to him.'

Boyd flinched from a blow that didn't come, then slumped in Dalton's grip.

'If you want me to do that, it'll just be quicker to kill me here.'

'All right.' Dalton ripped back his fist.

'Stop!' Boyd glared up, his eyes wide and beseeching. 'Don't hit me no more. I'll show you where Stirling is.'

'You should have said that in the first place.' Dalton released his hold, letting Boyd tumble on to his back. 'It'd have saved you some pain.'

CHAPTER 12

With the sullen Boyd at his side, Dalton rode out of Yellow Creek.

To Boyd's orders, they headed through Devil's Gully, the main trail south.

Ten miles out of Yellow Creek, the gully ended and Boyd pointed to a tumbledown shack, a quarter-mile out on to the plains. The walls were animal hides. Several boulders and an overturned buggy littered the collapsed corral at the front. From the closeness to the trail, Dalton reckoned it might once have been a trading post before the railroad had moved the centre of trade.

'How do you know Stirling is there?' Dalton asked.

'Raphael told the stage driver to stop here on the way to Yellow Creek. Stirling was there. He spoke to him then carried on.'

'And I guess,' Dalton mused as he dismounted, 'that was when Stirling told him about me.'

With Boyd at his side, Dalton slipped into the ditch at the side of the trail and followed it until he was level with the old post. Dalton peered over the side of the ditch, choosing the best route to the post, then glanced at Boyd with his eyebrows raised.

'I ain't helping you,' Boyd muttered. But when Dalton glanced at his fist, he raised his hands. 'But I ain't getting in your way either.'

With that promise being the best Dalton could have hoped for, he slipped from the ditch and snaked along the ground on his belly. Boyd shuffled along behind him until they reached the post where they stood on either side of the door.

Dalton mouthed a countdown, then kicked open the door and charged in.

Two paces in from the doorway, he stopped and arced his gun back and forth. A horse was by the back wall, but his gaze alighted on the man sleeping on the floor – Stirling Kimball.

Stirling jumped to his feet and turned at the hip, his hand swirling towards his holster, but Dalton bounded two long paces and kicked his gun hand away. The gun arced away from Stirling's fingers to slam into the wall, but Stirling danced back to stand free from Dalton.

'What you want?' Stirling said, eyeing Dalton's gun.

'Raphael's money.'

'I haven't got it.' Stirling spread his hands. 'Search me if you want.'

'Either way, you killed Saul Merrill. And I'm handing you in Sheriff Quentin to face that crime.'

'I didn't kill him. That was a bellboy at the Hotel

Splendour.' Stirling rubbed his brow, then raised a finger. 'He was called Ryan.'

In open-mouthed shock, Dalton stared at Stirling, his own surprise paralysing him.

Then a sharp thump on the shoulders knocked him to his knees. He half-turned to see Boyd standing behind him, his hands raised high and clenched together, ready to hit him again.

Dalton flinched away. Boyd's blow whistled by his left ear, but it still crunched into his shoulder and knocked him sideways.

Footsteps scurried towards him as Stirling advanced on him, and he rolled away, seeking to roll clear, but Boyd's rough hands crashed down on him.

Dalton flailed an arm, looping it around Boyd's chest, and the two men tumbled together. He looked up to see that Stirling wasn't heading for him, but for the gun he'd kicked to the side.

Dalton squirmed out from Boyd's grip, then slugged his jaw, crashing him on his side, then jumped to his feet and dashed after Stirling.

He pounded after him, but Stirling leapt and skidded across the floor to drag the gun into his grip, then turned on his back to aim up at Dalton.

'That's far enough,' he said, smiling.

Dalton skidded to a halt and raised his hands.

'Ain't no need for that. I saved you once before. And that should mean plenty to an innocent man.'

For long moments, Stirling stared up at Dalton, then climbed to his feet.

'I guess it does.' Stirling rolled the gun into the

back of his hand and swung it into his holster.

'You can't let him go,' Boyd whined, from the floor. 'He wants to ruin everything.'

'And if he does, I will kill him.' Stirling pointed a firm finger at Dalton. 'But for now, my debt to you is repaid.'

Still facing Dalton, Stirling grabbed his horse's reins and walked it around him, then to the door, but when Boyd moved to follow him, Stirling raised a hand.

'Hey,' Boyd whined. 'I'm coming with you.'

'I got no use for a loser like you.'

'I ain't a loser. I lured Dalton here.'

'And,' Stirling snorted, 'from the looks of the bruising on your face, you're not very good at luring either.'

Stirling led his horse through the door, leaving Boyd standing before the door with his hands on his hips.

'He don't know nothing about gratitude,' he murmured.

Dalton sauntered to Boyd's side and slammed a hand on his shoulder.

'You're right there. And you don't know nothing about keeping promises.'

Boyd kicked at the dirt. 'I promised to take you to Stirling. And I did.'

'I guess you did.' Dalton glanced away, then swung back and clipped Boyd's jaw, tumbling him on to his back. 'But that's for jumping me.'

Boyd rolled to his feet and advanced on Dalton,

but Dalton raised his fists and the two men locked gazes. Boyd was the first to turn away. Dalton still watched him wander across the post to ensure that he wouldn't jump him again, then strode outside.

With his hand to his brow, he stared down the trail, but he didn't see Stirling.

For Stirling to have disappeared so quickly, he must have headed for Devil's Gully, but Dalton still strode out from the house and searched for his tracks. When he found them, he hunkered down beside them, tracing his likely route, which he reckoned led to the east of the gully.

A footfall sounded behind him, but Dalton just stood and strode to his horse.

Then a hammer clicked into place behind him, forcing Dalton to stop.

'Boyd,' he said, 'you did what I asked and took me to Stirling. I didn't ask you to jump me, but as far as I'm concerned, we're even.'

A harsh chuckle sounded behind Dalton, and it wasn't Boyd's voice.

'We will never be even,' the voice muttered.

Dalton winced and raised his hands to shoulder level, then turned.

Ten paces from the post, Hunter stood with his gun aimed at Dalton's head and his gaze firm. Behind him, his four men paced round from the back of the post and trained their guns on him, too.

'What you doing out here?' Dalton asked.

'I don't have to answer to you. But you have to answer to me. And this time, you'll give me that carpet-bag and a whole heap of money.'

Dalton edged sideways, keeping his gaze from the post, but then saw Boyd wander out from the back of the building. Boyd flinched, darted a glance at Hunter, then along the row of men flanking him.

'I don't know about that.'

'You do. Now, take off your gunbelt, or I'll shoot it off.'

Dalton kept his gaze on Hunter, but as he removed his belt and dropped it at his side, he swung round to ensure Boyd was directly behind Hunter.

But instead of helping him, Boyd backed to his horse, lifting his legs with deliberate care.

Dalton confirmed that Boyd was just going to escape and not help him, then raised his chin.

'At least I got someone to help me.' He looked over Hunter's right shoulder.

'You won't distract me.'

'All right,' Dalton said, raising his voice. 'Take him, Boyd.'

'Boyd ain't much use for anything but talking too much in saloons. He won't ever help you.'

Dalton glanced at Boyd who was now speeding his journey to his horse.

'Then it's a pity for you that he has a gun aimed at your back.'

Gus moved to turn, but Hunter raised a hand, stopping his movement.

'Don't rise to this man's bait. Boyd will run like the dog he is.'

'Boyd,' Dalton shouted, 'shoot him!'

Hunter's right eye twitched with momentary doubt and, at that moment, Boyd reached his steed. He raised his leg, the movement dragging a whinny from his horse.

Hunter flinched and glanced back to see Boyd leap on to the horse. He raised his gun, but Boyd lurched forward and broke into a gallop.

Dalton used the distraction to dash at Hunter. But the row of men turned on the spot to confront Dalton and Gus ripped off a shot that blasted a slug into the earth at his feet. Dalton still ran on, but Gus laid down an arc of lead that ripped grit into Dalton's ankles, forcing him to skid to a halt, then dance back to avoid the slugs.

'You sure can dance,' Gus gibbered. 'Do it some more.'

Gus, then the other men, blasted lead, but this time Dalton folded his arms and stood tall, ignoring the bullets pluming the earth around his feet.

Hunter raised a hand. 'Enough. He just ain't dancing. But he will talk.'

He gestured to Gus, who paced around Dalton and grabbed his arms from behind.

'I got nothing to tell you,' Dalton muttered.

'You were after Boyd Dooley. Then you were after Stirling Kimball. You got an idea where the money is. And you'll tell me.'

'You just summed up what I know. Boyd may have the money, or Stirling may have it, or then again somebody else may have it. Aside from that, I got nothing to say.'

Hunter shrugged. 'Soften him up. See how committed he is.'

Two men paced forward and stood on either side of Dalton, rolling their shoulders. The first man stomped forward and slugged Dalton deep in the guts, then followed through with a flurry of blows that would have flattened Dalton if Gus weren't holding him upright.

But when the second man stepped up and pummelled Dalton with a round-armed blow to the jaw, Dalton rolled with the punch, then kicked a leg wide. His sudden movement surprised Gus and, with his leg braced, he hurled Gus over his shoulder and to the ground.

The circle of men charged in to surround him, but Dalton only had eyes for Gus's gun and as Gus floundered, he lunged for the gun and ripped it from its holster, then pressed the barrel into Gus's stomach.

'Back off,' he muttered, 'or I blast him two.'

'You ain't ordering us,' Hunter snapped. 'We got you surrounded.'

'You have, but before you kill me, I'll take down Gus and then you.'

Hunter glared at Dalton, but then grunted and gestured for his men to back away.

Dalton waited until they were ten paces away from him and stood, still keeping his gun aimed down at Gus, then paced to his own gun.

With the belt looped over his shoulder, he edged sideways to his horse, but as he moved to mount it, the man at the end hurled his hand to his holster and thundered lead at him. The bullet whistled past Dalton's ear, but Dalton swung back and blasted a slug into the man's chest, knocking him back and around.

In a lithe action, Dalton leapt on his horse. Hunter and the other men went for their guns, but when Dalton thrust the reins to the side, he hurtled straight for them and not away.

At a gallop, he bore down on them.

Hunter just had time to blast off a wild shot then leapt to the side in self-preservation.

Two more men scattered from Dalton's advancing horse but one man stood his ground, aiming up at Dalton. He blasted off one high shot. Then Dalton was on him. His horse's hoofs pounded the man into the ground, the man's broken cries dying as Dalton charged away and down the trail.

He fired a speculative shot over his shoulder, but by then Hunter and his men were dashing for their horses. At a gallop and 200 yards back, they followed, but Dalton headed straight into Devil's Gully.

Then, at the first bend, he pulled to the side and took cover behind a boulder.

Two minutes later, Hunter and his trail of men hurtled into the gully.

But they kept going.

Dalton waited and when they rounded the next bend, he emerged and backtracked, directing his horse along the line of hoof-prints they'd made in entering the gully. He didn't expect this ruse to slow them for long, but after his journey here, his horse couldn't outrun them all the way back to Yellow Creek, and he needed somewhere to make a stand.

He looked back frequently, but he returned to the post with still no sign of Hunter emerging from the gully, so Dalton dismounted and led his horse through the door.

He patted the horse's rump, encouraging it to go all the way in, then kicked the door closed.

'You are under arrest,' a voice said.

Dalton swirled round to find that a man stood in the corner of the post.

And it was Deputy Vaughn.

CHAPTER 13

Vaughn smiled as he walked towards Dalton with his gun raised.

'Guess you're going to shoot me here,' Dalton said.

Vaughn snorted, then bent to collect a coil of rope from the ground, but Dalton broke into a run. He pounded across the earth, getting to within three paces of Vaughn, but then Vaughn blasted a low slug, the lead ripping past Dalton's thigh.

Dalton hurled himself through the air, his arms thrust out, and hit Vaughn full in the chest, sending his gun flying, and bundled him on to his back.

Vaughn skidded across the dirt before ploughing to a halt.

But Vaughn kicked up with both feet and bundled Dalton up and over his head, Dalton's momentum letting him fly through the air before he landed flat on his back.

He lay, stunned, then shook his head and jumped

to his feet. He swirled round to find Vaughn also staggering to his feet, but he didn't give him time to regain his footing and charged him, leading with his right shoulder, and barged him back three paces.

But Vaughn set a foot back and skidded to a halt, then hurled both his arms up and grabbed Dalton in a neck-hold.

The two men strained for supremacy, both men trying to loop their legs around the other man's leg and tumble him to the ground, but they both kept their footings and they swung round on the spot.

Vaughn was the first to entangle his leg and make Dalton stumble. Then he hurled him to the ground. Dalton sat up, ready to throw himself at Vaughn again, but met a vicious kick that slammed into his chin and flattened him.

He lay, his vision whirling, then staggered to his knees, but when his eyes focused, he saw Vaughn staring at him, his recovered gun aimed at his head.

'You reckon you can . . .' Dalton strained his hearing.

Outside, hoofbeats heralded a rider approaching the post.

Vaughn snorted and firmed his gun hand.

'Perhaps this is the time to end this. Taking you to justice might be too much trouble.'

'Then you'll die here, too.'

Vaughn cocked his head to the side.

'You reckon that's Hunter returning?' He watched Dalton nod, then shrugged. 'His type don't worry me.'

'He should, and the two of us will stand a better chance.'

'We'll never work together.'

Outside, firm footfalls paced towards the door.

Vaughn darted his gaze back and forth between the door and Dalton, then swung round to keep them both in view.

Then the door hurtled back, a firm foot knocking it open.

In the doorway, Sheriff Quentin stood.

'What you want?' Vaughn muttered, glancing at Quentin from the corner of his eye.

'I'm Sheriff Quentin, and I want to know what you're doing.'

'I'm taking this man with me.'

'You ain't.'

Vaughn snorted, then swung his gun away from Dalton to aim it at Quentin, but Quentin hurled his hand to his holster and ripped off a shot, wheeling the gun from Vaughn's hand.

Vaughn spun with the blow, then staggered round to face Quentin, wringing his hand.

'You just made an enemy today, Quentin.'

Vaughn thrust his hand beneath his armpit, wincing, and hunched over, but when Quentin gestured to Dalton to join him, Vaughn swung up, a previously concealed weapon glinting as he swung it out from his jacket.

'Watch out!' Dalton shouted.

Quentin winced, then swung round, ducking with the movement. Vaughn's shot from the small pistol whistled over his head but, hunched over, Quentin ripped lead into Vaughn's guts, knocking him around, to his knees, then on to his belly.

Quentin checked where Dalton was standing, then holstered his gun and stalked sideways to Vaughn. He hunkered down beside him to feel his neck.

He nodded then, with a hand under each of Vaughn's armpits, dragged him through the doorway.

'Obliged,' he said, looking up at Dalton as he passed.

'Just a pity you didn't kill him.'

'I don't shoot to kill, not when I still want to know why he was trying to kidnap you.'

'I got no idea.'

'You got no idea,' Quentin intoned, 'even though he has a deputy's badge and he's crossed over the state line.'

Dalton sighed. 'It's a mighty long story.'

'And you'll have plenty of time to tell me.' Quentin paused in his backward journey. 'Because you are under arrest.'

Quentin pushed Dalton towards the cell beside Ryan's and, with a sigh, Dalton backed into it.

'You ready to tell me that long story now?' Quentin said as he swung the cell closed and locked it.

'Why don't you ask that man why he wanted me?'

'Because Doc Stone is getting a bullet out of him and he'll be out cold for some time.'

Dalton shrugged. 'Even when he comes round, you won't get much of an answer, because he didn't have much of a reason.'

'And that's why I won the battle to arrest you, and why you'll face my charges.'

'Which are?'

'I ain't sure yet. But you've been close to Stirling twice. And twice is twice too often for my liking.'

'I forced Boyd to take me to Stirling, then tried to capture him so that I could prove Ryan's innocence. None of that is suspicious.'

'*All* of that is suspicious.' Quentin sighed, then beckoned Dalton to come to the front of the cell. He lowered his voice to a whisper. 'And did you find anything to prove Ryan is innocent?'

Dalton glanced into the adjoining cell to see Ryan looking at him, his eyes wide, but Dalton shook his head.

'Nope,' Dalton said. 'I found nothing to prove he's innocent.'

CHAPTER 14

'I hoped I wouldn't see you in here, Dave,' Ryan said.

'I tried to avoid it.' Dalton wandered across his cell and shrugged. 'But I was unlucky.'

'Were you helping me?'

'Yeah, but don't remind me.'

Ryan stared up at Dalton, but Dalton sat on his bunk and faced the front of his cell, so Ryan rolled off his bunk and wandered to the wall closest to Dalton.

'Dave,' he said, his voice low and demanding, 'what's wrong?'

'Nothing.'

'Then why won't you talk to me?'

Dalton rolled over on his bunk, turning his back on Ryan. He pulled his hat low over his eyes and tried to induce sleep. After the exertions of the last few days, he was exhausted, but his mind whirled with the problems he faced.

Within a few minutes, Ryan relented from pestering him, and by degrees, he slept.

It was dark outside when Deputy Swanson's sliding of a dinner plate into his cell awoke him.

He sat on his bunk and stared at the stale bread and hard, salted beef. But as he pushed these uninviting offerings around his plate, he found that his former irritation with Ryan had subsided enough for him to look over his shoulder and into Ryan's cell.

'Your food any softer than mine?' he asked.

'No, but I'm glad you're speaking to me now.' Ryan sighed. 'And I'm obliged to you for trying to help me. And I hope you aren't in here for long because of me. But that's no reason for you to ignore me.'

'It ain't.' Dalton squared his jaw, trying to force himself to stay quiet, but then, with an angry slap of his fist against his thigh, he swirled round on his bunk to face Ryan. 'But the fact you killed Saul Merrill is.'

Ryan flinched. 'I didn't kill Saul. Stirling shot him when he had a better hand.'

Dalton waggled a firm finger at Ryan as he searched for the right words.

'But you are hiding something. And I reckon that's . . .' Dalton sighed, then nodded. 'The stake on the table was one hundred dollars. And you stole it.'

Ryan gulped. 'I *took* it. I had the best hand, except nobody noticed that after Stirling killed Saul.'

Dalton lowered his head, then rolled from his bunk. He paced across his cell to face Ryan through the bars.

'And why not admit to that?'

'And let Stirling Kimball know that I took his money?' Ryan mimed a knife drawing across his throat. 'I'd sooner have everyone think I stole Wallace's money than that.'

'Having everyone think you stole Wallace's money will keep you in a cell for a long time.'

'Better jail than death.'

'Stirling ain't that . . .'

Scratching sounded behind Dalton. He laid the plate on his bunk and glanced at Deputy Swanson to ensure he wasn't looking at him, but the lawman was sleeping under his hat with his feet on his desk. Then he searched for the location of the scratching.

'Rats?' Ryan asked.

'Got to be,' Dalton said, on hands and knees, peering under his bunk.

'Can't see them.'

'They're the worst kind.' Dalton sat and poked a lump of congealed gristle around his plate. 'It can't be the food that's attracting them.'

The scratching came again. Then something nudged Dalton's arm, gentle and insistent. Dalton flinched and batted the irritation away, but as he swirled round, he saw that it was a rope dangling through the cell window above his head.

Dalton glanced into the office, confirming that Deputy Swanson was still snoring, then stood on his bunk and glanced outside. In the dark, he saw nothing.

But then two hands gripped the bars and, with a grunt of effort, a florid face appeared at the window.

'Boyd,' Dalton whispered, 'what are you doing?'

'Breaking you out of jail,' Boyd whispered, 'that's what I'm doing.'

'Why?'

'Be quiet, or you'll wake Swanson, and I won't be doing any breaking out.'

'Just tell me why.'

'Shut up and tie the rope to the cell window.' Boyd dropped from sight.

Dalton glanced at Ryan, who bit his nails, then provided a reluctant but encouraging nod. So Dalton tied the rope to the cell bars, then paced back from the window.

The rope tightened. The cell window bars creaked and protested, then the whole wall shook.

With a grunt, Deputy Swanson clattered his feet down from his desk. He dashed to the cell, seeing the rope straining at the window.

'Don't do anything stupid, Dave,' he shouted.

Dalton raised his hands. 'I'm just watching what's happening, like you.'

The rope slackened, then pulled tight again and, in a great shower of dust and stone, the window exploded outwards, ripping half of the wall with it.

In the office, Swanson swung his gun from its holster and aimed it into the cell at Dalton.

'Stay there,' he muttered.

Dalton shrugged and, one pace at a time, Swanson backed to the office door, but when he was twenty feet away, Boyd hissed an urgent command from outside. Dalton still waited for Swanson to back another two paces then, when Swanson glanced through the window, Dalton thrust his head down and charged at the hole.

Swanson ripped off a shot, the slug cannoning into the cell bars and ricocheting behind Dalton but, by the time he'd fired a second time, Dalton was leaping through the hole.

Outside, Boyd had unhitched the rope attached to the cell window from his horse and was releasing a second horse. Dalton pounded to that horse. As he mounted it, Swanson dashed from the office.

Along the road, the commotion had forced people out on to the road, but everyone had the sense to stay back from this jailbreak.

Swanson shouted a warning, but Boyd blasted off an arc of gunfire that sent him scurrying back into the office. Then, side by side, Dalton and Boyd galloped out of Yellow Creek.

Both men concentrated on hard riding and headed for Devil's Gully. Dalton aimed to hide in the place in which he'd hidden from Hunter earlier, but Boyd had the same sort of idea and directed them to a tangle of rocks, one hundred yards in from the gully entrance.

They both dismounted, and while Dalton secured their horses, Boyd returned to slap away their hoof-prints with a branch.

Then they both melted back into the shadows.

Five minutes later, Deputy Swanson galloped by, a strung-out posse following. But each man had his gaze set on the trail ahead.

Even so, Dalton and Boyd stood in silence until the hoof-beats had receded. Then Boyd edged out and peered down the gully. He returned with a huge grin emerging.

'Well,' Dalton said, 'I'm mighty obliged, but seeing as you're the only one who knows why you've helped me, what we're doing next?'

'I want two thousand dollars. You want Stirling. And as Stirling has the two thousand dollars, I reckon we can help each other.'

'I can see that. But I don't see why you now want to go up against your old bosses.'

'I've had enough of them. Stirling treats me like trash, and I never get much reward from Raphael's schemes.'

'Schemes? You mean he's done this before?'

'Not on this scale, but Raphael has a method that works.' Boyd tapped his chest. 'But this time, I'll be the one gaining.'

'Trouble is, I can't let you do that. I need that money to prove Ryan is innocent.'

'Stirling will do.'

'Quentin wants him for the murder of Saul Merrill. He doesn't want him for stealing Wallace's money. Without it, Raphael gets the hotel, Wallace loses everything, and Ryan is still in jail.'

Boyd squared his jaw. 'Not my problem. Now, be quiet, or I'll send you back to jail.'

'But wouldn't you like to see Raphael behind bars and losing everything?'

'I would. But as I can't do that and get the money,

that won't happen.'

'But capturing Stirling is sure to fetch a reward. Then there's Wallace's gratitude. You could make plenty out of this without getting a wanted name for yourself.'

Boyd rubbed his jaw, then held his hands wide.

'How much?'

'If you help me, you'll get at least one hundred dollars.'

Boyd snorted. 'I ain't good with numbers, but two thousand is one hell of a lot bigger than one hundred.'

'And you ain't good at keeping out of trouble, but a live man can do more with one hundred dollars than a dead man can do with two thousand dollars.'

Boyd shrugged. 'I see your point. I'll think about it.'

Dalton considered Boyd, but with his new ally firming his jaw, he nodded.

'You do that. So, where are we going?'

'I lost Stirling's trail. I need help to find it again.'

Dalton nodded and followed Boyd. They headed up the side of the gully and, at a high spot, waited. An hour later, the posse returned to Yellow Creek.

Still, they waited another hour, but when they didn't see anyone else out searching for them, they returned to the gully and rode to the old post.

They picked up Stirling's tracks and followed them, finding two other sets of tracks later, Quentin's and Boyd's presumably, but they all disappeared a half-mile on when they reached a length of solid rock.

'This is where I lost them,' Boyd said, then gestured around, encouraging Dalton to pick their route.

'I ain't no tracker,' Dalton said, pulling his horse to a halt and peering down at the moonlit barren ground.

Boyd shrugged. 'Neither am I. But that's why I brought you along. You seem to know things about Stirling.'

Dalton nodded and headed his horse onwards while still peering at the ground.

'And so do you.'

'Not that much,' Boyd said, drawing alongside. 'Stirling never spoke to me much.'

'Why not?'

'He's a gunslinger. He had no need to even acknowledge me.'

'So, why did Raphael employ you if Stirling is as confident in his powers as that?'

'He wanted someone on his side.'

Dalton drew his horse to a halt. 'You mean Raphael and Stirling don't get on?'

'Nope. Raphael owes Stirling money.'

'How much?'

'Sixteen hundred dollars.'

'That's a mighty big coincidence,' Dalton mused, leaning forward in the saddle.

'Not really. Raphael's been working hard to raise the money to pay Stirling off.' Boyd chuckled. 'Well, when I say hard, I mean other people worked hard, and Raphael took their money off them.'

'And always the same trick?'

'Yeah. Raphael sets up a deal with the money apparently being in that carpet-bag. I have an alibi to be elsewhere, and—'

'And you find someone like me to take the blame when you switch the bags?'

Boyd nodded. 'Yeah, but that ain't important now. We got to find Stirling.'

Dalton rubbed his chin and peered ahead at ground that he could search for days without finding Stirling's trail.

'We have, but I can't see no tracks either.'

'Then if you were Stirling, where would you go?'

Dalton looked ahead, taking Boyd's idea and trying to imagine what Stirling would have done.

Then he snorted and glanced over his shoulder.

'Stirling needs to stay close to Raphael and be somewhere where they can meet easily.'

Boyd slapped a fist into his palm and grinned.

'I like easy.'

Dalton glanced back down the trail towards Yellow Creek.

'But that's the trouble. I reckon Stirling is in the one place where we just can't get him.'

CHAPTER 15

Four hours after the jailbreak, Dalton and Boyd headed down the boardwalk towards the Hotel Splendour.

They'd figured that nobody would expect them to return to Yellow Creek this soon after their jailbreak, but even so, they'd sneaked around the outskirts of town, then through the shadows.

This late in the evening, few people were on the road, and those who were didn't look their way.

Outside the hotel entrance, they looked up at the second floor. Dalton closed his eyes to remember the layout of the hotel rooms, then counted the windows and pointed.

Boyd followed his gaze. 'You reckon Stirling is in room seventeen?'

'Yeah, next to Raphael.' Dalton snorted. 'It used to be my room.'

'And mine,' Boyd murmured, passing Dalton a length of rope.

Dalton gestured for Boyd to give him room then

tried to lasso a projection above room eighteen's window.

On the first two attempts, the rope rebounded, but as Dalton was playing out the rope to retry, Boyd muttered that someone was approaching and the two men melted into the alley beside the hotel.

They stood quietly and watched two men head towards the saloon on the opposite side of the road.

When these men had passed, they swung out and, with urgency spicing his senses, Dalton lassoed the projection at his next attempt.

With a last set of instructions to Boyd, Dalton grabbed the rope and walked himself up the hotel wall. Half-way up, he glanced around, confirming that nobody was out on the road, but a hissed urge to hurry from below forced him to speed his journey.

At the window, he swung on to the windowsill and, using Boyd's knife, prised open the window.

The moonlight through the window let him see that the room was in the same state as it had been in when Raphael had surprised him, so he swung into the room, then tiptoed to the wardrobe in the corner. He opened the door and listened. In the next room, steady breathing sounded, so he slipped through the wardrobe and into the wardrobe in the adjoining room.

But through the gap in the doors, he saw only a thin sliver of light.

He took a deep breath, deciding that on the count of three he would kick the door open and leap out to take Stirling.

But then, outside in the corridor, a cough sounded.

'I'll check that noise out,' a voice said.

'No,' another man said. 'Check room eighteen. I'll check this one.'

Dalton strained his hearing and when the man spoke again, he recognized the voice as being Wallace's.

Rustling sounded within the room, as of Stirling arising from the bed and stalking to the door.

In the corridor, Wallace coughed again, then thrust the key in the lock and pushed the door wide.

Dalton jumped from the wardrobe to see Stirling charge through the opened door, a firm arm propelling Wallace away, then hurtle down the corridor. At his heels, Dalton ran through the door, but Wallace's flailing body rebounded from the wall and into him. The two men went down.

With much muttering, Dalton extricated himself from Wallace and dashed after Stirling. But when he reached the top of the stairs, Stirling was already at the bottom. Dalton bounded after him, taking the stairs four at a time, but Stirling was pushing through the front door as Dalton reached the floor.

Through the window, Dalton saw arms fly as Boyd jumped Stirling, but then the two struggling men tumbled away from the door.

Dalton hurtled across the room and through the door, but then had to leap to avoid the pole-axed Boyd who lay on his back, rubbing his jaw.

Dalton skidded to a halt and glared down the

road, seeing Stirling leap on a spare horse outside the next-door hardware store.

Behind him, Boyd leapt to his feet and pounded past him, but Dalton glanced into the road to see that Sheriff Quentin was striding purposefully towards them. Dalton dashed after Boyd and dragged him into the shadows beside the hotel door.

Boyd struggled, but then found that Dalton had stopped him.

'What you doing?' he muttered. 'Stirling's getting away.'

'He ain't got the money,' Dalton grunted, then pointed to the alley beside the hotel. 'And Quentin's coming.'

Boyd nodded and scurried into the alley, but Dalton swung back and slipped into the hotel to see that Wallace was heading to the front door.

'You,' Wallace muttered, sliding to a halt before the door. He raised his hands before his face. 'Stay away and don't hurt me.'

'I won't harm you,' Dalton said. 'But I do have to talk to you.'

'I ain't listening.' Wallace shuffled to the side, aiming to slip past Dalton. 'I'm fetching Quentin and he can deal with you.'

Dalton edged to the side to block Wallace's route.

'Quentin will be here in about fifteen seconds. But if you want to see your money again, you will help me avoid arrest.'

Wallace slowed to a halt. 'You reckon you can persuade Ryan to talk?'

'Ryan is innocent!'

Wallace snorted. 'What about that one hundred dollars?'

'He got that money from his poker game with Stirling Kimball, but he can't admit that or he'll have Stirling after him.'

Wallace shrugged. 'So, if Ryan didn't steal my money, who did?'

'Raphael Huffman.' The door behind Dalton opened. From Wallace's sigh of relief, Dalton assumed it was Sheriff Quentin, but he fixed Wallace with his firm gaze. 'And I'm the only one who knows where's he's hidden it.'

CHAPTER 16

'You did what?' Quentin muttered when he reached his office.

'I asked Dave to try and capture Stirling,' Wallace said, mopping his brow.

'And Ryan?'

'He won that one hundred dollars in a poker game.'

As Sheriff Quentin lowered his head, grunting his distrust of Wallace's story, Dalton glanced to the cells. Doc Stone had been bandaging a cut on Ryan's arm and was gesturing to Deputy Swanson to release him, but when the doctor passed Dalton, he smiled at him.

'What's wrong with Ryan?' Dalton asked Stone.

'Your jailbreak knocked a bar from the window and cut him.'

'The window bars didn't come loose.'

Stone shrugged. 'Then it must have been something else that cut him.'

Dalton nodded and turned to find that Quentin

was wandering by him to unlock Ryan's cell.

'I can go?' Ryan asked, jumping to his feet.

'Wallace's told me what happened at your poker game. And as that one hundred dollars was the only evidence I had, you can go.' Quentin watched Ryan wander into the cell doorway. 'Just stay in town while I finish my investigation.'

'And what about me?' Dalton asked.

'Wallace's paid for the damage to the cell.' Quentin glanced back at Wallace and sneered. 'I don't believe a word of his story, but it's enough to keep you out of jail – for now.'

With that begrudging acceptance, Ryan and Dalton left the office. On the boardwalk, Ryan shook Wallace's hand then drew in a deep breath of cool, night air.

'Obliged, too,' Dalton said.

'Don't be,' Wallace said. 'You made a promise, and I can change my story if you were lying.'

'I wasn't. But you do realize that we'll have to confront Stirling?'

Wallace gulped, but then stood tall.

'I guess I'll have to face up to him if I want my hotel back. I just wish there were another way than stealing money from a gunslinger.'

'Don't worry.' Dalton smiled. '*We* won't be stealing from him.'

'Come in,' Raphael said, to Dalton's knock.

Dalton wandered into room sixteen. Raphael was sitting at his writing-desk, his back to Dalton, but when Dalton just stood in the doorway, he turned and flinched.

'Howdy,' Dalton said.

'I didn't expect to see you again.' Raphael stood and faced Dalton. 'Once you'd escaped, I thought you'd never return to Yellow Creek.'

'But I thought some more about what you said.'

'Then I hope you haven't returned to . . . to do anything stupid. I gave you my word that I won't tell anyone about your identity, as long as you don't tell anyone about . . .' Raphael nodded to the door, and Dalton swung it shut. '. . . about anything that you know.'

'I'm not here to kill you. I just want to talk.'

Raphael spread his hands. 'Then talk.'

'You're seeing Stirling before sun-up.'

'I am.' Raphael's gaze flickered to the door to the adjoining room, and raised his voice. 'What of it?'

'So, you'll need a hired gun again.'

'Stirling is my business partner. I don't need protection from him.'

'Is that so?' Dalton wandered across the room to the door to room seventeen. He glanced at it, then leaned on the doorframe. 'But don't worry about Stirling hearing you. He's no longer next door. He hightailed it out of town. Did you not hear the commotion?'

'Yellow Creek is a bustling town. But he comes. He goes. Nothing has changed.'

'But it does mean that you can talk freely and admit you need protection from him.'

'And if that were so, why would I have employed Boyd? He was no match for a gunslinger like Stirling.'

'He wasn't. But he had one useful attribute.' Dalton smiled. 'He was expendable.'

Raphael chuckled. 'He was at that. And you're not?'

'No. But I *can* help you complete your transaction with Stirling.'

Raphael's gaze flicked over Dalton's shoulder, then down to meet Dalton's eyes.

'I may accept your help. But answer me this – why your change of mind?'

'I have no choice. I'm a wanted man, and a lawman is after me, except he's unconscious. But he'll come round soon and I need to lie low for a while. For that, I need money.'

Raphael stared at Dalton, then nodded. With his gaze never leaving Dalton, he leaned over the writing-desk and pulled it back from the wall. He hunkered down beside it, then tapped a projection on the side and raised the lid.

He reached inside and emerged with a bulging carpet-bag.

Raphael hefted the bag. 'Remember this – if you raise an alarm, I'll claim I'd just wrested this bag from you. As you're a wanted man and I'm a respected businessman, we both know who Quentin will believe.'

'And remember this – if I raise an alarm, you won't repay Stirling and he'll extract his fun out of you another way.'

Raphael snorted, then sandwiched the bag between two larger bags and headed outside.

Dalton had instructed Wallace to keep all the staff away and they left the hotel without anyone approaching them.

Side by side, they rode out of town. The night was cool. The low, full moon cast long shadows to their sides as they rode towards Devil's Gully.

'Just so I know what kind of trouble we'll face,' Dalton said as they rode into the gully, 'you want to tell me how you got involved with Stirling?'

Raphael didn't reply immediately, and when he did, his voice was reedier and less assured than it normally was.

'Three years ago, I got into a poker game with Stirling and couldn't repay my debt. To stop him killing me, I agreed a deal in which I'd double the amount I owed within a year.'

'And that was two thousand dollars?'

'That was eight hundred dollars. Except Stirling was so impressed that I'd raised the money, he gave me another year to double it again to sixteen hundred.'

'And you've raised that much?'

'Yeah. Two days ago, I tried to negotiate a lower deal, but when Stirling returned my eight hundred dollars, I went ahead with the . . . the purchase of the hotel before paying him the whole amount.'

Dalton nodded. He glanced into the moonlit hills, looking to the place where he and Boyd had hid out earlier this evening.

'So, why will he accept the money this time?'

'Sheriff Quentin knows he killed Saul Merrill. Stirling will have to move on now, and I reckon—'

A gunshot ripped through the air above Dalton's head, close enough for Dalton to hear it whistle by. As the echo faded, he glanced around, confirming that the shot came from the ridge at his side.

With a sharp gesture, he directed Raphael to dismount and head for a loose row of rocks that would protect them from above.

Dalton swung down from his horse and leapt behind cover, but Raphael loitered by his horse. Then a second shot ripped past, sending Raphael to scurry into hiding with him.

'Stay down,' Dalton snapped, pushing Raphael's head below the level of the rocks before them.

'Who is this? Nobody knows about this meeting but Stirling.'

'Boyd does,' Dalton murmured.

'He has a grudge. But he's a better aim than this man – even by moonlight.'

As Dalton nodded, Raphael jumped back up and edged a pace closer to his horse, but another gunshot ripped into the earth beside his feet and sent him scrambling back for cover.

Dalton bobbed up, glanced up the slope, then ducked and turned to Raphael.

'If you're worried that the shooting will spook your horse and your money will ride off with it, I'll get it.'

Raphael glanced at his horse, judging the

distance, then nodded. So, on his haunches, Dalton edged out from the rock, backing away from the direction of the shooting to give himself the maximum time under cover.

Then, ten feet from the rock, he dashed out and swung the bag from the horse's back.

A solitary shot ripped over his head, but he dashed back to his cover with the bag slung over his left shoulder.

A shot blasted into the earth, a few inches from his foot and instead of leaping behind the rock to join Raphael, Dalton dashed around the rock and stood before it. There, he dropped the bag to the ground and blasted six quick and wild shots into the hills.

He stood, reloading and searching for their opponent but, in the poor light, saw no movement. He grabbed the bag, which was lying back against the rock, and vaulted the rock to join Raphael.

'Any luck?' Raphael asked.

Dalton shook his head and settled in for a long stand-off.

For the next thirty minutes, he traded sporadic gunfire with their hidden assailant.

With each passing minute, Raphael became more agitated, even glancing at his watch, then at the sky, until he turned to Dalton.

'It'll be sun-up in an hour,' he muttered. 'He has us pinned down and Stirling doesn't like people who keep him waiting. We have to run for it.'

Dalton bobbed up again, and when their assailant

didn't return fire, he nodded and passed the bag to Raphael.

On the count of three, they leapt to their feet and dashed to their horses.

On the run, Dalton fired over his shoulder, then mounted his horse and, with Raphael ahead of him, galloped down the gully.

A short burst of gunfire blasted from behind, but all the shots were wild, and Raphael and Dalton thrust their heads down and concentrated on hard riding. They swung round the first bend, then continued at a gallop through the winding gully.

At each bend, they glanced back, but no pursuit was coming and, by the time they were approaching the end of the gully, both men were pulling back on the reins and slowing.

On leaving the gully, they stopped and looked back, but the gully was still and quiet.

With a nod to each other, they rode at a fast trot to the old trading post where they dismounted and, after one last glance at the gully, went inside.

Stirling sat at a table facing the door. He glanced at Raphael, then turned his gaze on Dalton.

'Dalton,' he murmured, 'I've repaid my debt to you. So, if you have any wild plans, you won't live long enough to act on them.'

'I know that,' Dalton said. 'But this meeting ain't about you and me. It's about you and Raphael.'

'Yeah,' Raphael said. 'This is the last time we'll see each other.'

'That depends,' Stirling said, pointing a firm

finger at Raphael, 'on whether you have *all* my money this time.'

'I do – every last cent.' Raphael raised the carpet-bag and patted the side, then threw it on to the table. 'Now, my debts to you are repaid.'

Stirling glanced at the carpet-bag, then fingered the handle.

'But I can't help but think that if I gave you another year, you could double the amount again.'

'Stirling, this closes my debts to you.'

Stirling flicked the handle away and narrowed his eyes.

'Your debt closes when I say it does.'

'Then just say it. I'm staying in Yellow Creek as the owner of the Hotel Splendour and that's a town you'll never revisit, not after you killed Saul Merrill.'

Stirling glanced at Dalton. 'I didn't kill him.'

Dalton shook his head. 'Quentin knows the truth.'

'So,' Raphael said, 'it'd be easier on you if you just moved on.'

'It might, but perhaps one day, when everyone's forgotten what I did, I might return and want somewhere to stay where a friendly hotel-owner will feed me the finest food and drink.'

'Even if I owe you nothing, I'll always give you that. But take the money.'

Stirling firmed his jaw, then reached for the bag. He dragged it towards himself then raised it off the table, hefting the weight.

'Feels heavy enough.'

'It's more than heavy enough. I originally owed

you four hundred dollars, and I've doubled that, twice. And I'm repaying you the original money, too. Now, we got no reason to continue this.'

Stirling opened his hand to let the bag thud on to the table.

'You do want to end this mighty bad. All right.' Stirling fixed Raphael with his steely gaze. 'Your debt to me is settled.'

As Raphael heaved a sigh of relief, Stirling ripped the bag open and peered inside.

Stirling's eyes narrowed. His right hand twitched with a momentary tremor.

'What's this?' he roared.

'The payment,' Raphael said. 'Two thousand . . .'

Stirling thrust a hand into the bag and extracted a handful of cut newspaper.

'You were trying to play your bag-switching trick on me.'

'I wasn't,' Raphael gasped. He glanced at Dalton who edged a pace closer to the table. 'The money—'

Dalton kicked out, knocking the table into Raphael's chest and fluttering the cut newspaper in all directions. He swirled round, not waiting for Stirling to regain his senses, grabbed Raphael's arm, then hurtled for the door.

Raphael resisted a moment, then let Dalton drag him away. They'd just reached the doorway when, with a huge roar, Stirling hurled the table from him.

Both Dalton and Raphael dived through the doorway, the action saving them from a burst of gunfire that ripped over their heads.

They rolled outside, then to their feet and dashed for the nearest cover, an overturned buggy.

They dived for cover as Stirling stormed into the doorway, but when Dalton rolled to a halt, Raphael grabbed his collar and dragged him close.

'I know what you did now,' he grunted. 'While Boyd pretended to ambush us in the gully, you switched the bags.'

Dalton licked his lips, then nodded.

'Yeah. I thought you might appreciate the irony.'

Raphael glanced over the side of the buggy, but a gunshot ripped into the wood before his face, forcing him to duck. He turned to stare into Dalton's eyes, then snorted.

'I can't appreciate anything when Stirling is trying to kill me.'

'Then appreciate this. I didn't steal your money, because it's Wallace's money now.'

Raphael sighed and released Dalton's collar, then slumped down to lean back against the buggy.

'I don't care. I won't get out of this alive and neither will Wallace once Stirling works it out.'

'Don't worry. I have a plan. Boyd did help me swap the bags, and now he's heading here to help us.'

'Your plan to save us is Boyd Dooley?' Raphael winced as Dalton nodded. 'That has to be the worst thought-out plan I've ever heard.'

'Don't panic. He'll have Ryan and Wallace as back-up.'

'A bellboy and a nervous hotel owner. This isn't filling me with confidence.' Raphael glanced up to peer at Stirling's position.

Stirling blasted at him again, the lead ripping into the buggy and sending splinters flying around him, but Dalton only had eyes for the three riders galloping down the trail from Devil's Gully – Ryan, Boyd and Wallace.

The riders galloped the last thirty yards, then jumped down from their horses and fanned out, using the shadows in the hollows and ditches around the post for cover.

Dalton lifted a moment to wave them in, then blasted covering gunfire at the post which forced Stirling to leap back into the building.

On the run, Boyd and Ryan reached him, and Wallace arrived a moment later, clutching another carpet-bag.

When all three men were safely hidden behind the buggy, Raphael glanced at each of them with his lip curled in distaste.

'I hate your plan,' he said, glancing at the carpet-bag. 'You just got us all killed to steal my money.'

'My money,' Wallace murmured, then glanced at Dalton and waved his gun with a shaking hand. 'But he's right. I'm no use with a gun. I'm a hotel owner.'

'You know how to shoot it?'

'Yeah.'

'Then when I give the order, just aim at the post and keep on firing. You might get lucky.'

'And if I don't?'

'*We* might get lucky.'

Wallace nodded, but his hand shook with an involuntary tremor and he had to bite the hand to still it.

Dalton issued orders to Boyd to head to a boulder on the other side of the doorway so that they could shoot at Stirling from two positions. Then Ryan and Dalton jumped up and blasted gunfire at the post.

As Boyd hurtled for the boulder, Wallace caught on and blasted at Stirling, too, and the sustained gunfire kept him pinned down in the building.

'What now?' Wallace asked when Boyd gained cover.

'The more directions we can fire at Stirling, the better.' Dalton pointed to a boulder that was square on to the door, then turned to Ryan and patted his shoulder. 'You ready to go for that boulder?'

Instead of nodding, Ryan stared over Dalton's left shoulder. Dalton furrowed his brow, but then turned.

The first hint of sun-up was lightening the horizon, and framed against the sky, three men were riding down the trail.

Dalton narrowed his eyes, then winced.

The approaching riders were Hunter and his two remaining men.

CHAPTER 17

'We got you trapped,' Hunter shouted as he dismounted fifty yards from the post.

'We got a good position,' Dalton shouted.

'It won't help you none.' Hunter and his men scurried behind cover – the boulder that Ryan was previously going to head for. 'And hey, Stirling, we ain't after you.'

'Don't care,' Stirling bellowed. 'I don't have partners.'

'Me, neither. But Dalton has the money. I reckon we ensure he doesn't keep it, then decide whether we're splitting it equally, or the other way. In the meantime, I ain't looking to take you out.'

Stirling dragged the table into the doorway and hunkered down behind it.

'Understood.'

A ferocious burst of gunfire ripped into the buggy, coming from both Stirling and Hunter.

'We're going to die,' Wallace whined with his

hands over his head and splinters splaying all around him.

'Nothing's changed,' Dalton murmured. 'We still have Boyd in a good position.'

'Boyd isn't trustworthy.'

'While we have the money,' Dalton said, glancing down at the carpet-bag, 'he's the most trustworthy man I can think of.'

'Trouble is, the money's got Hunter's attention, too.'

'It ain't. There's something he wants more than the money – me.' Dalton pushed the bag to Ryan, then raised his voice. 'Hey, Stirling, I wouldn't trust Hunter. He was helping me to find you earlier, and if he hadn't—'

'Don't listen to him, Stirling,' Hunter shouted. 'He's trying to distract you.'

'Now,' Dalton whispered, then leapt to his feet.

Ryan and Wallace swung up and blasted gunfire at Stirling and Hunter while Dalton dashed at an angle to Hunter's position, aiming for a hollow twenty yards to Hunter's right.

Boyd joined in and the covering gunfire forced Hunter and his men to stay down. But, just as Dalton closed on the hollow, one of the men jumped up. Boyd ripped a slug into his chest that knocked him back and around to fall over the side of the boulder, his arms dangling.

Dalton dived into the hollow, rolling over his shoulder as he slammed to a halt on his back, then swung round and, on hands and knees, scrambled back. Gunfire was ripping out from all the hidden men, but by degrees, it slowed.

'Hey, Hunter,' Dalton shouted with his head down, 'you ready to give in yet? You ain't cut out for this.'

'You'll pay for that taunt, Dalton.'

Gunfire sounded again, and Dalton bobbed up, but it was to see Hunter hurtling the last few paces to his position. Dalton ripped his gun up, but he wasn't quick enough and Hunter barged into him, tumbling him on to his back.

They hit the ground, entangled, but with Hunter's weight blasting all the wind out of Dalton's body, Dalton couldn't muster the energy to keep Hunter's hands off him and Hunter wrapped both of them around his neck.

On his back, Dalton glanced left and right, looking for help from either Boyd or Ryan, but this position was hidden from both men. And, with the gunfire that was blasting out beyond the hollow, Dalton reckoned Stirling was keeping both men pinned down.

Then Gus skidded into the hollow to join them but, on seeing Hunter pinning Dalton to the ground, he chuckled and rolled back on his haunches.

'You want me to shoot him?' he gibbered.

'I'm going to squeeze him to oblivion,' Hunter grunted, veins popping out on his forehead as he tried to close his hands into one giant fist.

Dalton grabbed Hunter's arms and tried to prise them apart, but with flickering lights surrounding him and his vision darkening by the moment, he could only squeeze with an ever-weakening grip.

With no choice, Dalton let his hands go limp. He gulped in the barest of breaths, then threw all his strength into bucking Hunter from him.

His lunge failed, but Hunter's grip did waver, letting Dalton drag in one more tortured breath. With a hint of strength oozing into his limbs, he bore down, then thrust up his legs, kicking Hunter in the back and tumbling him forward.

Hunter sprawled over him, but his hands did slip away from Dalton's throat.

Dalton pushed to the side, tumbling Hunter away, but Gus aimed his gun down at him.

'Now?' he asked.

Hunter rolled clear, then snorted.

'Yeah,' he muttered. 'Kill him!'

Gus grinned then firmed his gun hand. In desperation, Dalton leapt to the side. Gus's shot blasted into the earth just inches from his right hand.

On his side, Dalton kicked out, arcing a huge gout of dust at Gus. Most of it missed, but enough dirt lanced into Gus's eyes and his second shot also blasted wide as he blinked his blindness away.

Dalton rolled to his feet and lunged for his own gun. The weapon cleared leather, but before he could swing it round to turn it on Gus, Hunter grabbed his arm and thrust it high.

Dalton and Hunter crashed into each other, the gun swinging over their heads. An involuntary finger twitch wasted a shot in the air as, beside them, Gus swung round, blinking the dust away, then firmed his gun hand and aimed the weapon at Dalton's exposed side.

A gunshot blasted.

Dalton winced, but it was Gus who staggered a pace, then fell to his side. Dalton glanced around but saw Boyd standing on the side of the hollow, early morning light rippling through the smoke rising from his gun barrel.

But then another gunshot ripped out. Boyd screeched, then tumbled to his knees and on to his front, a gunshot wound reddening his back.

With anger hurtling through his veins, Dalton rolled his shoulders, then slugged Hunter away. As Hunter staggered back a pace Dalton slammed a round-armed blow to his jaw that sent him tumbling.

Even before Hunter had slid to a halt, Dalton had trained his gun down at him, but Hunter gave him no choice. He threw his hand to his holster.

Dalton fired, ripping a single slug into Hunter's forehead.

Then, with his lip curled in distaste at what Hunter had forced him to do, he dashed to Boyd's side and rolled him over.

Boyd peered up at him, a smear of blood on his lips, his watery gaze suggesting he was as confused about his bravery as Dalton was.

Dalton patted his shoulder then leapt to his feet and, with rage fuelling his stride, charged at the post. He pounded across the ground, aiming directly for Stirling's position.

Stirling leapt up from behind his covering table and, at that moment, Dalton threw himself to the ground to skid across the dirt on his belly.

Stirling fired. The slug ripped Dalton's hat from his head, but on his belly, Dalton steadied his aim. Then Stirling swung round, redness exploding from his shoulder and with him half-turned away, Dalton blasted lead into his side. Stirling hunched over and staggered back a pace, then swung his gun down towards Dalton, but a second shot to the neck wheeled him into the post.

Dalton lay a moment, ensuring that Stirling wouldn't re-emerge, then rolled to his feet and glanced at the buggy.

'Who winged him?' he asked.

'I got lucky,' Wallace said, then glanced at his gun and mopped his brow. 'I just got lucky.'

Dalton nodded. 'And so did I. Where's Ryan?'

'He went around the back of the post to try and outflank Stirling.'

'I'll check he's all right. You help Boyd.' Dalton glanced at Raphael. 'And you just sit there, and don't steal Wallace's money.'

'Ryan has my money,' Raphael whined.

As Wallace hurried to Boyd's side, Dalton dashed around the back of the post, but, on failing to see Ryan, entered the post through the back door.

Inside, he saw Stirling lying dead by the door. Beside him, Ryan was hunched over the two carpet-bags. He pulled out a bundle of bills, snorted, then flinched on seeing Dalton.

'Stay away, Dave,' he muttered, throwing the bills back into the bag.

Dalton glanced at the strewn newspaper, then at Ryan's hunched posture.

'You ain't planning on doing something stupid, are you?'

'Nope. I'm thinking calmer than I ever have.' Ryan rolled the bag on to his left shoulder and turned to Dalton, revealing the gun in his right hand. He aimed the gun at Dalton.

'Don't, Ryan.'

'Why shouldn't I? Stealing one hundred dollars is just as much a crime as stealing two thousand.'

'Sheriff Quentin knows you didn't steal the one hundred.'

'And that'll change now.'

'Stirling is dead. He can't deny the truth about what happened at the poker game.'

'I don't care about that poker game.'

Dalton narrowed his eyes. 'What you trying to tell me?'

'That I lied. I didn't get the money in the poker game. It was like everyone said.' Ryan kicked the bag at his feet, cascading the cut newspaper across the floor. 'I stole that one hundred dollars from this bag.'

'You're not that stupid.'

'And I guess I am. I didn't plan to do it. But I was standing in that corridor, waiting for Wallace. And I had more money than I'd ever seen in my whole life in my hand. I took a handful off the top. I thought maybe nobody would notice. But I wasn't to know the rest of the bundles in there were just newspaper.'

'You were tempted. That don't make you a thief.'

'But Raphael knows there was some real money in that bag, and when Wallace finds his payment is short, everyone will know the full story.'

'Then do the right thing now. Put the money back and nobody but us will ever know about it.'

'You—'

'What's happening here?' Wallace said from the doorway behind Ryan.

'Nothing,' Dalton said. 'Ryan was just checking that all the money is still in the carpet-bag. Ain't that so, Ryan?'

CHAPTER 18

Wallace wandered into the post and took the bag from the unprotesting Ryan. With his right hand pressed to his chest, he hefted the bag.

'Mighty glad I now have that,' he said.

Ryan and Dalton exchanged a long stare, but to Dalton's encouraging nod, Ryan forced a smile and they filed outside.

Wallace had dragged Boyd to the buggy, and even Raphael was fussing around him.

'If this is over,' Boyd said, his voice weak, 'when do I get a reward?'

Dalton hunkered down beside him.

'Now, and I guess the only question is – who should pay you?'

'Don't look at me,' Raphael murmured. 'I got no money now.'

'But you have. If the money was never in that carpet-bag, Wallace still owns the Hotel Splendour.'

'But I might be prepared to sell it to you,' Wallace said, smiling. 'If the price is right.'

'I am not renegotiating that,' Raphael snapped.

'If you don't want me mentioning your double-dealing to anyone, you will.'

Raphael glared at Wallace, but then gave a reluctant nod.

'I am prepared to provide another two hundred dollars.'

'One thousand, and you'll give me free board whenever I want. I fancy being pampered.' Wallace chuckled. 'I reckon room sixteen might become my usual.'

'You will always be welcome,' Raphael grunted, each word uttered through clenched teeth. Then he held out a hand.

Wallace glanced at the hand, then shrugged and slugged Raphael's jaw with a sharp uppercut that snapped his head back and, as Raphael staggered back a pace, slugged him deep in the guts, bending him double.

As Raphael staggered round on the spot, Wallace rolled his shoulders. And when Raphael had completed a full circle, he threw back his fist and hammered his cheek with a blow that slammed him to the dirt.

Wallace stood over him, waiting for Raphael to rise, but when Raphael slumped on to his back, he straightened his jacket and turned.

'Now,' Dalton said, 'that was the right way to do business with a double-dealer.'

Wallace chuckled his agreement then hunkered down beside Boyd.

'Raphael might not come up with an appropriate

reward,' he said, 'but once we get you patched up, I'll be a rich businessman in need of a hired gun. You interested?'

Boyd provided a weak nod, then livened up sufficiently to start negotiating his terms.

Ryan drew Dalton aside.

'I'm sure Raphael won't talk about either of us,' he said, 'but I'll stay on in the hotel to check that he doesn't.'

Dalton patted Ryan's arm. 'Obliged.'

'But I guess you'll be moving on?'

Dalton turned to look down the lightening trail, then nodded and headed towards his horse.

'Yeah,' he said over his shoulder. 'I can't risk seeing Sheriff Quentin again or waiting until Deputy Vaughn comes to.'

'You can't.' Ryan hurried to walk alongside him. 'But don't—'

'Hey,' Wallace whined. He waved the last bundle of bills from the carpet-bag. 'I'm twenty-five dollars short.'

Dalton glanced at Ryan. 'I thought you'd replaced the whole one hundred dollars.'

Ryan shrugged. 'Maybe not all of it.'

'Ryan, you got tempted, but this time . . .'

'I know, I know. But I have to pay Doc Stone for that whiskey he's been feeding Vaughn. It's sure kept him knocked out so far.'

Dalton laughed and grabbed his horse's reins.

'Obliged. How much did twenty-five dollars pay for?'

'By the time the money runs out, you should be well over the state line.'

'I hope so.' Dalton mounted his horse and turned it towards the trail. 'But I reckon that for a wanted man, there can be no peace.'

'Perhaps.' Ryan stood back. 'But with the help of good friends, occasionally a wanted man can earn a respite.'

Dalton exchanged a smile with Ryan. He directed a tip of his hat to Wallace and Boyd, and a sneer towards the comatose Raphael, then hurried his horse on.

Ahead lay the long trail south, and perhaps a place where a wanted man could secure a more permanent peace.